A Thin Line Between

Happily Ever & After

A Novella written by D. D. Miles

Dedication

To everyone that has enjoyed this book series, I dedicate the final book to you. Thank you for coming along for the ride.

Acknowledgments

First giving all honor and glory to God, I'd like to thank my mother, Janice Williams for her loving support. It's not every day that you have an avid reader, who so happens to be a retired Language Arts teacher, at your disposal. So if my subjects and verbs do not agree, or perhaps you come across some misspelled words, blame her. I'm just kidding, but thank you, mommy, for everything. You are priceless. To my dad, Larry Gosha who is my cheerleader and so supportive. I thank you, dad, for everything as well; your encouragement matters greatly. Thank you to my family and friends for your support as well. As you can see, I can't take full credit for any of this. I am so grateful to those who have come into my life to inspire and motivate me. To you, I say thank you as well.

To the Reader: I thank you for taking out the time to read this novella series. You're just one page away from an explosive romantic drama. Let's Go!

Chapter 1

BENJAMIN

Something terrible must have happened here,
because when I attempted to pull into Living Well's
parking lot, I couldn't. Police cars and news cameras had
blocked off and filled the parking lot. I ended up parking in
the lot of another building that was a block down. I tried to
call Stacey to see what was going on, but my call went
straight to her voicemail.

"What the hell is going on?" I asked aloud while
walking toward the building. There were even more police
cars arriving at the scene. As I got closer, I could hear a
woman sobbing, but couldn't see who it was because the
police officers had surrounded her.

Just as I was getting closer to the front door of the
lab, I saw Detective Bennett coming from the group that
surrounded the woman, crying.

"Detective Bennett?" I called out to him.

"Mr. Harris, how are you, sir?"

"At the moment, I'm okay, but what's going on here?"

"Someone kidnapped an infant."

"Oh my God, that's crazy! What is wrong with people? That would explain the crying that I heard. I'll be praying for the family. I knew something horrible had happened when I saw officers everywhere. I'm here to take a paternity test. Do you know if the lab will reopen? Better yet, I'll just reschedule my appointment." I said, reaching for my phone.

"No, we have officially closed the lab, and it will remain closed until the investigation is complete."

"I fully understand. We'll have to make an appointment somewhere else. Thank you,-"

"Detective Bennett, you may want to take a look at this." The officer said, interrupting me and showing him something on a tablet. "Does she look familiar to you?" He asked the detective while they watched the video.

"That's her! Mr. Harris," he called. "Can you look at this and tell me if you recognize this person?"

I looked at the video and was at a loss for words. The woman whose sobbing I heard was now standing in front of me. "Yes sir, I do. This is Kherington." I told him while watching Stacey.

"Sir, do you know how she would know that you would be here today?"

"No sir, I wouldn't. I have no idea." I answered.

"You mean to tell me that you know the woman who kidnapped my baby!?" Stacey shouted in my face.

"Ma'am, we understand that you are upset and rightfully so, but attacking Mr. Harris is not going to help matters." The detective said as he stood in between us.

"This is all your fault. You had her kidnap my baby!" She yelled while being restrained by a man who was failing at keeping her calm.

"Stacey, I had nothing to do with this. Kherington is a mentally ill woman who is not thinking clearly, and hasn't been for quite sometime."

"I told you he was not your son," she said, sobbing in the arms of the man comforting her.

"Mr. Harris, can you meet us at the precinct? We need a statement from you?" Detective Bennett asked.

"Sure, I'll meet you there."

"Benjamin Harris, you had better get me my baby back. If that bitch harms him in any way, I'm going to hold you personally responsible." Stacey threaten.

"Stacey, I promise I will do everything in my power to bring your son home." I told her.

"Our son, I am Cameron's biological father, Andrew Lassiter." He said, extending his hand to shake mine.

"I promise you both that I will do what I can to bring Cameron home." I said, shaking his hand.

"Anything that you can do to help us bring our son home, man, I would greatly appreciate it." He told me while Stacey was talking to another officer. "Stacey told me why you wanted the test, and I feel like this is my fault because she didn't want to come. Man, if you could see my little guy, you'd know he's mine. He looks just like me. I just feel so bad about all of this."

"This isn't your fault, man, believe me. There's a lot to this story and without making things harder for you guys, I'm going to leave it right there, but you have my word. I'm going to do my best to bring Cameron home."

***

I was sincere in my promise to them. I just wished I knew how to reach Kherington to convince her to bring the baby back. I believed Andrew when he said Cameron was his son, and it breaks my heart to know that his life was in danger. I wish I could say Kherington wouldn't hurt him, but she had killed before. So what's stopping her now, even if it's an innocent child?

I called Tamara to tell her the latest.

"Hello."

"Hey babe."

"What's wrong with you? You sound off."

"You're not going to believe this," I said.

"What happened now?"

"Kherington struck again."

"How?" She asked.

"More like who. She kidnapped Stacey's baby."

"Wait, she did what?"

"Yep. She tricked her into registering for a phony paternity test."

"Wait, I'm confused. How does she even know Stacey?"

"I confided in her about how Stacey was giving me the runaround about the paternity of the baby. I'm guessing she took things into her own hands by pretending to be from an actual lab. Kherington called Stacey to set-up an appointment, and when they arrived, Kherington pretended to be a nurse that worked there and escaped out the backdoor with the baby."

"Oh, my God!" She yelled out.

"Oh, and it gets better. Detective Bennett was there and now I'm headed downtown to give another statement."

"I know Stacey isn't one of my favorite people, but I wouldn't wish this on anyone, not even her."

"I hear ya. What concerns me is we don't know where she could have gone. It's like she disappeared right into thin air."

"This is very scary. Did you tell her about Phillip?"

"No! When I was talking to Cameron's actual father, I told him it was more to the story, but didn't elaborate."

"You met Cameron's actual father?" She asked.

"I did. He was just as devastated as Stacey was. My heart goes out to them, babe."

"Wow. It definitely does. I can't believe this."

"This has gone from bad to worse. Hold on a sec." I said, looking to see who was calling on the other line. "Yeah, I'm back. I'm so tired of people calling me from spam numbers. No, I don't want your health insurance, car warranty, nor do I have student loans. This needs to stop."

"Those calls are aggravating, especially at a time like this."

"Tell me about it. Well, babe, I just pulled up to the precinct. Do you have plans for this evening?"

"Nothing major. I am going to go visit Erica when I leave here. What's up?"

"I wanted to take you to dinner tonight?"

"Dinner is fine with me. Just give me the time and location and I'll be there."

"I can't pick you up? You know what, never mind. I'll send you the details when I leave."

"Okay, I'll see you later." She said, hanging up.

I knew not to push the issue of picking her up. I'm just glad she had actually accepted my invitation. Here lately, we've been cordial, but nowhere near where we once were. I take ownership of that. I wanted my wife back, and she wasn't giving me any signs of returning, no matter how hopeful I was.

Chapter 2

KHERINGTON

Again with this Ben? Why won't you answer my calls? "Aww, come here, my sweet boy. I was just calling daddy to let him know that you were safe and sound, and that I was taking really good care of you. He is going to be so excited to finally meet you. That mean old lady was keeping you away from him. Yes, she was. I can't wait until we are all finally together. We're the perfect family, me, you, and daddy. Once I get you squared away, I'll try to call him again."

Our sweet baby boy was perfect. He stayed asleep while I drove an hour out of town. I didn't think Stacey was going to buy the whole idea of coming in to take the test. She had turned me down for weeks, but out of the blue she agreed, and I knew it was only a matter of time until my plan came together. She may have birthed my love's first child, but denying him the chance to be a father was her worst mistake. That's not how a surrogate should behave.

I can't blame her, who wouldn't want to love on this beautiful child. I was there when she delivered him. I stood in the background, and watched our surrogate until he crowned, but I stepped out of the room before anyone noticed me. I waited near the nursery until his nurse stepped away to get more supplies. That's when I snuck my first peek. Through the window I watched the most beautiful baby I'd ever seen. It was love at first sight, and I knew what needed to be done next. Through his medical records, I was thankful to learn that he was not being breastfed, but was on a special type of formula. When placing my orders, I made sure that I had more than enough of it. I even bought those special bottles to prevent ear infections. I couldn't bear to have my baby in all that pain. I read many books on what to expect as a first time mother, and felt like I was well prepared. I even bought and altered his birth certificate to reflect Benjamin and I as his parents, and purchased him a social security card. He had just had his first round of immunization shots and wouldn't need the next set for another four months. By then, his looks would have changed greatly, and no one would ever suspect a thing.

Ben and I were finally getting the family that we both deserved. Together, we will raise our son with love, but first he needs to answer the damn phone so that I can tell him about it.

Chapter 3

TAMARA

Today was Erica's baby shower, and we all were looking forward to this distraction. Between Ben feeling guilty and Stacey going out of her mind with worry, being stressed was an understatement right about now. So far, there were no leads regarding Kherington and the baby, and all the police could do was wait until she makes a mistake. When I say the psycho had covered her tracks, she had. I don't know if the FBI was shocked or impressed by how she had slipped away. They did an extensive background check on who they were dealing with. I supposed to them, a normal person couldn't possibly do the things she'd done, and get away, but a psychotic person is capable of doing almost anything. She had all of us fooled, everyone except Phillip, but she silenced him permanently before he could tell anyone else.

"Hey beautiful, what has you lost in thought today?" Marcus asked.

"I'm sorry. I'm just thinking about the mess we're in."

"That fault belongs to one person, and you're not her. As hard as it will be, focus on Erica and the baby. They both need your support." He said, holding my hand.

I nodded okay to him, but also locked eyes with Ben, who was not pleased to see Marcus here. What was I supposed to do? Erica invited him to come. "It looks like everyone is here. Let's get this party started." I said. I stood thanking everyone for attending and I recognized the grandparents, aunts, and uncles and called them A'ja's future babysitters.

Whoever Erica hired to decorate for her did an amazing job. The decorator used chocolate, magenta pink, soft pink, and rose gold balloons to decorate the space, adding brown plush teddy bears throughout. It was simply beautiful.

Out of all the games played, the baby food testing game was the best. All the brave men that wanted to play sat at the same table. They had ten unlabeled jars of baby food in front of them to taste. The one that guessed the most correct matches won. TJ didn't last three rounds before bowing out.

"Something is seriously wrong with y'all to keep going." He told the other men. "Ben, go ahead and quit, bro."

"Leave me alone. I got to focus." Ben said.

"Ce, you good, dawg?" TJ asked.

"Un-uh." Ce replied.

"Marcus, how about you?"

"I'm hanging in there, bro," Marcus replied.

"Un-huh, I forgot. You'd probably had worse." TJ said, laughing.

Marcus stuck his tongue out and threw up his hook just like an Omega man would and kept writing. The rest of the men were locked in and tried to concentrate on the task before them.

"TJ, will you leave them alone? You just don't want to lose by yourself." Erica said.

"Hey babe, we're not giving A'ja none of this stuff to eat," He said, pushing the jars back.

"What is she supposed to eat then, TJ?"

"Some pot liquor and cornbread. Just like I did."

"Some what? Not my baby. I don't think so." She said.

"Girl, you don't know nothing about that kind of good eating. Only someone raised in the South would know about that. See, you're not southern-bred and that's why it's over your head."

"Un-huh, the way that it sounds, I should be glad that I missed out." Erica said, laughing.

"Times up!" I yelled. "At this time all spoons and pencils should be down." I told them. I went to each participant and checked their lists. And found that we had a clear winner. "The winner of this contest is JJ!"

JJ was so excited to hear that he had won. He was full of smiles as he jumped around in celebration.

"Wait, how he won? He can't even write or spell." TJ asked.

"Un-huh daddy. I did won. I tasted it and told Mr. Marcus what it was." He said proudly.

"You sure did, big man." Marcus said, giving an excited JJ a fist bump.

"Nah, nah, nah, y'all cheated." TJ declared.

"They should be disqualified," Ben mumbled.

"Really, you're that sour, bro? You'll stoop so low as to take a prize from a little kid, really?" Marcus asked Ben, who was glaring back at him.

Tension between the two of them was so apparent that Ce had to step in.

"Congrats nephew," Ce said after high-fiving JJ. "Be cool. This is not the time or the place." He said to Ben, who had not stopped glaring at Marcus.

"That's what's up." Ben responded to Ce. "Congrats, little man." He said, rubbing JJ's head.

"Uncle B, you mad cause I beat you?" JJ asked while eating his third cookie and laughing.

"Boy what? Unc isn't mad at you. I could never be mad at you." He said, grabbing him up. "Are you going to split your prize with me?"

"Nope." He said, squirming and laughing.

"Now see, I got to beat you up."

"Daddy help me." JJ said, laughing and reaching out for his dad.

"Nah buddy, you're over there rocking and winning with somebody else. Didn't even help your pops out. Come on B let's DDT him." He said, referencing an old wrestling move.

"Alright, if y'all are finished horse playing with JJ, we're getting ready to open gifts." I said.

"That's code for come and help lift the heavy stuff." TJ whispered to Ben.

Baby A'ja was one blessed little girl. We were in hour two of opening gifts, and were down to the last. I read the card out loud as I did the others.

Congratulations Erica and TJ,

I wished I could be there,

but as a busy mom myself,

I hope this gift brings your

little sunshine as much joy

as it has mine.

Love Always,

Auntie Kherington.

I said, dropping the card out of my hands. It was like someone had hit me with a stun gun because I stood there trembling.

"Don't open that gift!" Ben ordered, then calling the police.

"Are you okay?" Marcus asked, rushing to my side.

"I'm okay, just shocked. How did she-" I was trying to ask but couldn't finish.

"Come sit here." Marcus directed me to the nearest chair.

Chaos ensued. I felt so bad for their guest because many didn't know what was going on, or had any idea of the danger that we were in. For those that did, fear was shown across their faces. The security team bomb rushed into the room and removed the gift and card from the floor. This was too much.

Chapter 4

BENJAMIN

We were already on the edge and for Kherington to send a baby shower gift, said that torment was the name of the game that she chose to play. Per usual, I answered the same questions that is often asked regarding her, "No, I haven't seen or heard from her." I was beginning to sound like a broken record at this point. I'm just tired, and to add to my frustration was an innocent baby. Instead of sitting there feeling hopeless for myself, I directed my attention to the emails that needed my immediate attention and quick response, but I couldn't shake this nagging feeling that kept tugging at me that something wasn't right. Plus, someone keeps calling me from a spam number. At first I thought it was a telemarketer, but they kept calling at odd hours of the night. There was no way this was a telemarketer calling on a Sunday night after ten o'clock. So I answered.

"Hello!" I yelled into the phone.

They hung up without saying a word. I don't know what else to do at this point. This would be the sixth number that I've blocked. I have other things better to do than to play on the damn phone. If I have my number changed, that should help with these issues. Calling my phone provider will be the first thing I do on my agenda tomorrow.

I was reading an email from our corporate accounting department that captured my attention. They were requesting verification of some transactions that were made on our corporate account. The only three that had access to cards from that account were Phillip, Tamara, and myself. The transactions had to be from Tamara's card for the foundation. I hadn't used the card for anything, but I'll look over the transactions and see. There were multiple Amazon transactions listed. Surely Tamara hadn't done this. But I needed to check with her first before I had the account flagged for fraud.

"Hello." She said.

"Hey, did I catch you at a bad time?"

"Nah, I'm just getting ready for bed."

"Really."

"Ben, what do you want?" She asked. I could hear Tamara's smile in her voice.

"Besides you?" I asked, trying to shoot my shot.

"I know you're not calling me this time of night about something you know you're not going to get."

"Girl, you were a sip away from coming home with me that night we went to dinner."

"And I quickly regained my senses."

"Senses, okay. You know you want to be with me. I don't know why you're doing this. Why are you still over there, and your boy was about to get messed up at the baby shower. Why was he there, anyway?"

"There it is." She said.

"There what is?"

"The truth."

"The truth?" I asked.

"Yeah, you almost caused a scene Saturday because you can no longer have your way."

"I can admit that I got heated. Some random man was holding my wife's hand and comforting her, and I shouldn't be bothered by that?"

"Oh, he's random now, okay?" She said.

"We're not going to go back and forth with who was right versus who was wrong. I take full accountability for everything that has happened, and it hurts me to my core to understand that I lost my wife, a good friend, and someone's child behind all of this. This burden of guilt that I have, weighs a ton. I've literally lost control of my life, Tamara, and there's nothing I can do about it. You're living with your ex, Phillip is dead, and Cameron's been kidnapped all because of me. And I can't take much more of this." I said, frustrated.

"Ben, you can't blame yourself for what Kherington has caused."

"But if I hadn't been so consumed with being a father, you wouldn't have ended up in Phillip's bed."

"That was on me, not you. I chose to do that. I looked for validation in someone who was not my husband, and when you tried, I shut you out. So if anything, it was me that caused her to fall over the deep end."

"I wished I could take it all back." I confessed.

"I do too, Ben, but all we can do is pick up the pieces and move forward."

"That's just it. Are we picking up our pieces together, or are we going our separate ways?"

"That's the question that I wrestle with on a daily basis." She said.

"I see. I'm sorry to pour all this out on you."

"I get it and understand. It's a lot to deal with."

"For my on mental health, I'm thinking about going to counseling." I told her.

"I think that's what we all need to do. This has been traumatizing for everyone."

"Tell me about it. I'm not going to keep you. I know that you were getting ready to go to bed, but have you made any Amazon purchases with you corporate credit card? I received a verification email from accounting."

"No, I haven't purchased anything from Amazon since Christmas, and that was from my personal credit card."

"I'm checking the card numbers against this report, and it's not my card. Do you know what your card number ends in?"

"Let me check." She said and confirmed her numbers afterwards.

"Wait, let me see something. I'm checking to see if this is Phillip's card number. I totally forgot to cancel his business credit card. So much has been going on."

"That's an understatement."

"Oh, my God! His card is being used as recent as yesterday." I confirmed.

"That's her! It has to be her," Tamara said.

"You're right. Who else could it be? I have to hit the detectives up, ASAP."

"Let me know what you find out."

"I'll be in touch. Goodnight." I said, hanging up.

Chapter 5

TAMARA

Dinner with Ben the other night was great. It reminded me of when we first started dating, that is, before all the drama ensued. The food was good. The wine kept flowing, and I was a bad decision away from making a horrible mistake. The man had me going. He was looking good and captured by full attention by wearing the cologne that I loved. I was in trouble and I knew it. Not only was he looking good and smelling good, he was also talking good. He took me back to the time when things were exciting and new between us. Ben could always take my breath away. He had swept me off my feet, but I remembered how quickly things had changed. I chose not to lose sight of the decisions we'd made along the way that led us here, broken-hearted and living apart.

"Hey, I saw that your light was still on." Marcus said, bringing me out of my thoughts. "Is everything okay?" Marcus asked. He'd just come in from wrapping up another twelve-hour shift.

"I'm okay, just got a lot on my mind, but what else is new with me these days? Enough about me. How are you?" I asked, deflecting. "How was work?"

"It was work. You know we stay busy. I'm afraid if they don't get control of the gun violence in this city, we won't have many more patients left to treat."

"Is it getting that rough out there?" I asked.

"Is it? Man, it just gets to me sometimes. Don't get me wrong, I love what I do, but my God, when will it ever end? If I never see another young man lose his life to senseless violence, I'd be a fortunate man."

"I hear you, but you can only help one person at a time."

"I do what I can for all of them. It just wears thin sometimes."

"That's understandable." I said, thinking about what Ben said to me earlier.

"So what else is going on in your world?" He asked, leaning against the doorframe.

"Nothing really. I spoke to Ben tonight." I told him.

"Oh, how did that go?" He asked dryly.

"It went okay. He was just talking about how things were going with him, and there maybe a break in finding Kherington."

"Really," he said, coming into the room and sitting on the bed. "That's good! What happened?"

"Someone has been using Phillip's business credit card to make Amazon purchases."

"That has to be her." He said.

"That's what we said too, but he is having it investigated."

"What about the gift from the baby shower?"

"The police have it, and we haven't heard anymore about it. But it makes me wonder if the gift came from Amazon too." I said.

"I'm wondering how did it get there? Did she deliver it herself, or was it sent by courier?"

"I can answer that. A courier delivered it there an hour before the shower. The site manager received and signed for the gift, and placed it on the gift table."

"That would explain why it was the last gift." He said.

"Yep, as people came in, they stacked their gifts on top."

"Unbelievable." He said.

"I'm hoping the police can piece all of this together and find her location."

"Me too. I know you are ready to get back to living your life."

"I am. This has really put things on stand-still, my marriage, moving, well, everything except the foundation."

"What about your marriage? What do you plan to do? Not to add to your full plate, but your husband acted like he was about to crash out during the baby shower."

"I know. It's just a big mess at this point."

"I'm sure the problem is that you're here with me. That's why I asked what were you planning to do about your marriage."

"To be totally honest, I'm not sure. I feel like so much has happened between the two of us that we need to let it go, but on the other hand, I was just as wrong as he was."

"What about me?" He asked.

"What do you mean?" I asked confused.

"You never thought about how your being here has affected me? I don't want to pressure you one way or the another, but you know how I feel about you. The only move I'm waiting on you to make is from this room to mine. I want to be the one to hold you until you fall asleep. I want to be the one to make you feel safe at all times. So whenever you're ready, you know where to find me." He said, standing to leave before kissing me on the forehead.

"But Marcus, I-"

"Tamara, there's no pressure. We have time, trust me. I'm just letting you know my thoughts." He said, before walking out of the room, leaving me more confused than I already was. Pressure was pressure, and I felt that thing heavy. Just like I heard him loud and clear. I knew I had to make a decision when Ben and Marcus's egos decided to flare. I knew what Ben's look meant when he saw Marcus holding my hand. Ben just knew he had no right to confront me about it.

Chapter 6

BENJAMIN

The detectives called us in for a meeting to discuss the investigation and their findings so far. It had been a while since we had any updates. I know Stacey had to be going through it. Hopefully, there had been a report of a sighting.

"Good afternoon, ladies and gentlemen. We called you all here to update you about what we know so far. Because this has been upgraded to a high-profile case, we wanted to inform the family and other interested parties of where we were currently in the case before releasing this information to the public. Updating you this afternoon will be Officer Randall."

"Good afternoon. The full autopsy and forensic report has returned, and it states the victim's toothbrush, the glass that was found next to the victim's body, and the bottle of alcohol found on the table were all laced with arsenic trioxide. Which also agrees with the cause of death reported by the medical examiner." He said.

"At this time, we now know the suspect in question may have visited the funeral home where the victim, Phillip Gray, was being funeralized." Detective Bennett stated. "We have video to confirm a woman dressed in all black, wearing a large hat, and shades matching the description of Kherington Draker provided by the FBI. On her visit, the alleged assailant signed her name in the visitor's book and kissed Phillip Gray's cheek before leaving. They confirmed that she also bought a floral arrangement leaving a card behind that read, "You were loved." The victim's family possessed the signed card left behind, and the FBI used handwriting analysis to compare it with other documents she had previously signed, confirming her identity."

Hush and shock filled the room.

"The baby shower gift and packaging were both tested for poisons. The lab found that there were zero traces of any harmful chemicals associated with the specimen. The package came from the distributor sealed. The gift's purchase address belonged to the business account of the deceased card holder, Phillip Gray. Someone sent other purchases to an Amazon locker an hour outside of town. We have turned all of this information over to the FBI," Detective Bennett said. "They will be in touch with the family to provide more information as necessary. If you have any questions, please don't hesitate to contact myself or Detective Rogers." He said before ending our meeting.

I wanted to talk to Stacey and Andrew before leaving, but Stacey was too distraught to speak to anyone. The meeting, in my opinion, was a complete waste of time. It shed no light on where Kherington and the baby could have possibly been. Nobody vanishes into thin air. An hour outside of town could've been in any direction.

I understand they couldn't give us everything, but give us something. I felt horrible for his parents. This meeting was mainly about the evidence that was being accumulated on Kherington. Nothing about a sighting, nothing about a lead. Nothing. Yes, learning that the baby shower gift and card weren't poisoned was a relief, but what could Stacey and her family do with that information? Nothing.

I was just as angry and frustrated as they were. None of this made any sense to me. Why call us to a meeting and not tell us anything helpful? I called TJ to relay the information about the gift.

"Hey, what's up, bro?"

"Besides pissed. Nothing much."

"What happened?" He asked.

"You remember me telling you about my having to attend a meeting today concerning the case. Well, it was almost a complete waste of time."

"What? How so? I thought the whole idea was to provide y'all with information."

"Yeah, man. That's what I thought too, bro. The only good thing that came out of it was finding out the gift you all received from Kherington was not harmful."

"We were wondering about that. I'll tell Erica, she'll be relieved. That's all she's been talking about since it happened."

"I just wanted to holla at you and let you know. I'll get back up with you a little later on."

"Alright."

"One." I said before hanging up.

Chapter 7

KHERINGTON

"My little man is so sleepy." I said to him. "You're such a wonderful baby. After I put you down for a nap. I'm going to call your daddy back. Those bad people on the news are telling lies about your mommy, and I don't want your daddy believing them. Calling me dangerous. I could never hurt you. You're my little light and bliss. I only hurt those that hurt me first. Yes, I do. If I see your surrogate mother across my television screen one more time crying and slinging snot, I may have to send her something to quiet her for good. I'm so sick of her. She's the bad one, not me. Had she'd done right by daddy, you wouldn't be here with me, now would you? No, you wouldn't. That's it, go to sleep, precious one." I said, rocking him to sleep.

I had to make a pharmacy list. I needed medicine for these terrible headaches I've been having. They're becoming almost unbearable. The slightest noise intensifies them. Aspirin helps for a moment, but it doesn't last long. I need something stronger, but that would require a prescription. Plus, I couldn't take anything that would make too sleepy to care for the baby, so I had to figure out something else fast.

I made my list for what I thought would do the trick and placed my order online to be dropped off at my Amazon locker before attempting to call Ben again. The last time I called, he yelled in the phone, and I had to hang-up. I'm doing well for now, but if my head starts to hurt, I'll have to hang-up again.

The last number I used, I believed he blocked. My calls were going straight to voicemail. I had many burner pre-paid phones. Whenever he blocks me on one, I go to another. Let's see if I'm going to get luck today.

"Hello." Benjamin said, answering.

"Hey baby." I said, trying to hide my excitement.

"Kherington, is that you?!" He shouted.

"Yes, I've been trying to call you, but-"

"Where are you? Where is Cameron?!" He
yelled.

"There you go yelling at me again."

**"Kherington, this is serious. I need to know
where you are!"**

**"What you need to do is stop yelling at me. I can
hear very well."** I yelled back almost waking the baby.

"Kherington, I'm sorry for yelling. Please tell me
where you are. Where's the baby?"

"Is that all you care about is the baby? What about
me?" I asked.

"I care about you, too. I just need to know where
you all are."

"I didn't call you to discuss that. I called because-"

"What do you mean? Where are you?" He asked,
interrupting me.

"This may have been a bad idea." I told him.

"Kherington, wait!" He yelled.

Was the last thing I heard Ben say before ending the

call. It appeared that Ben had believed what had been

reported on the news. I would have argued my case, but my

head had started to hurt badly.

Chapter 8

STACEY

"Come on, baby, eat something for your granny."

She said, sitting on the edge of my bed.

"Big Mama, I'm not hungry." I told her.

"I know, but I need you to keep your strength up so

you can be strong for my baby when he comes home."

"She's right babe. You have to stay strong for Cam.

He needs you more than anything. I need you. So sit-up and

eat your soup," Andrew said.

"I miss my baby." I told them as I slid further down

in the bed.

"We know you do, dear, but listen, we are believing

God that He is going to return that baby back to you safe

and unharmed. And you must believe it, too." My

biological father, Richard said.

"And once you finish this soup. I want you to get out of this bed and take a shower. I've already laid your clothes out in there for you like I did yesterday." Big Mama said.

"Thanks Big Mama." I said, but did not move. I knew it was better to agree with her than to argue.

"Come on twin. Just eat a little bit." Tracey said.

I was too weak to move. I feel like my heart had been ripped out of my chest, and all they can talk about was me eating food. For what? How could my eating bring my baby back? It wouldn't. My heart was gone, and so was my desire to eat. All I could do was hold my baby's teddy bear and cry.

I've done all that I could do. I went on television, passed out flyers, everything, still nothing. Yesterday, I learned the worst news possible. My baby had been taken by someone who was wanted for murder. A murderer had my baby. I blamed everyone for this. I blamed myself. I blamed Ben. I even blamed Andrew for suggesting that we go. I was mad at the world and all I wanted was my child back. We sat in that room yesterday and learned absolutely nothing about where he could possibly be.

I was beyond devastated. I was so overcome with worry and grief that I could no longer sleep. All I could see when I closed my eyes was my baby crying out for me, and there was nothing I could do to help him. He doesn't know that woman. I don't know if she's mistreating him or worse. How is my baby being fed? Is she even feeding my baby? I'll eat when I know my baby can, otherwise they can miss me with that. Until I knew that my baby was alright, I would not be. This grief was more than any parent should have to endure. No matter what, I will never stop looking for my baby. He was all that I had. He was all that I wanted. I would give my last breath just to have him back in my arms.

Chapter 9

BENJAMIN

Pop opened the church and asked us to all come together for a prayer vigil for Baby Cameron. The community came out in droves to support the family. Stacey looked disheveled. As long as I've ever known her, I've never seen her like this. The few pounds the baby added were now gone, and more. I wanted to speak to her but as soon as I walked up she cut a look my way that said keep your distance, and I consented. I know she blames me and I fully understand why.

"Hey pop." I spoke.

"Hey son. Where's Tamara?" He asked.

"I'm not sure, pop. I spoke with her earlier, but she hadn't said whether or not she would be coming."

"That's unfortunate. I was hoping to see her." He said.

"Let me see if I can call her." I said, before stepping away. "Hey babe, pop is looking for you. Are you coming to the prayer vigil tonight?"

"Nah, I wanted to stay home and chill tonight." She said.

"Oh wow, we're both in for a disappointment. I was looking forward to seeing you tonight. Maybe we could've gotten dinner or something later."

"Boy, that's all you like to do is eat." She said, laughing.

"So you do remember." I told her, smiling.

"Bye, Ben." She said, laughing.

<Smack.>

"How dare you!" Stacey said after slapping me. **"Standing up here, laughing and having a good time?"**

"Girl, have you lost your damn mind!?" I yelled as pop tried to hold me back.

"This is all your fault!" She yelled.

"I'm good, pop." I told him. I was pissed, but I wasn't going to put my hands on her.

"What in the world is going on?" Pastor Billingsley asked, trying to help pop.

"Hey Doc." Pop said. "It's just a misunderstanding, man."

"Why is she blaming Benjamin?" He asked, looking at me.

"Because she's crazy as hell. Make this be your last time hitting me, too." I said to Stacey.

"Benjamin!" Pop yelled.

"Hey man, I know what she did wasn't right, but you don't have to talk to her like that. She's going through a lot," Andrew said, stepping to me.

"I meant what I said. She needs to get her emotions in control." I said to him.

"Okay fellas. Let's not do this. There are too many people watching you all." Pop said. "The media outlets are here with their cameras and everything. We don't need to add anything else to this already devastating situation. We are not here for this. We are here for the baby, and that's it."

"Andrew, please, son. Pastor Harris is right. We don't need this. Please take Stacey and you two go and have a seat over there, and we'll get started shortly." Pastor Billingsley suggested. "Please, son."

"Yes sir," he responded, still watching me.

"Benjamin," pop said, motioning for me to take a seat. I picked my phone up and took my seat, still pissed off.

"Lawd help us." Pastor Billingsley said to pop.

"You can say that again. How do you know Stacey and her family?" Pop asked.

"She's my daughter."

"Excuse me? She's your what? Wait, I know your wife and your two daughters. Hold on, I must have heard you wrong.

"No, you me heard me right." Pastor Billingsley said.

Huh?" Pop asked, confused.

"Man, it's a long story, but she is in fact my daughter." He said.

"It's longer than you think. We were almost in-laws." Pop informed him.

"Nah, you don't say? So those two were engaged?"

"Not at all. She was engaged to my other son, Christopher. But they called off the engagement when it was found out that she had an affair with Benjamin."

"Wait, what?" Pastor Billingsley asked with his mouth hanging open.

"Doc, the stories I could tell you about those two will turn your hair fifty shades of gray. Sir, when I tell you that you haven't heard anything yet, please believe me."

"I'll see you Monday afternoon if you're available." He told pop.

"I'll be right here."

***

After leaving the prayer vigil, I received another email about verifying another purchase that was made as recent as today. The police asked me not to close the account. They were using it to track Kherington's location. I reviewed the numerous transactions made. Whatever she had planned was for their survival. She had several purchases back to back. That's what caused the fraud alerts. I could only hope that she had ordered enough baby formula, pampers, and wipes to open her own store. If I knew this, that would let me know that Cameron was doing okay. I knew the purchases had to be delivered. I just didn't know where. The police already had some information, but she just ordered something else and it's from the Amazon pharmacy. By the purchase price this was in a large quantity. Wherever she was, someone was not well, and that puts the baby in more danger than before.

Chapter 10

STACEY

My family and I were waiting for the agents to arrive with new information regarding my baby. I could barely hold it together. It had been weeks with no information, and when I heard something, it was about how dangerous the person was who had my baby. This can't be my life. To think about the extremes she went through to do what she did left me speechless for days. If I weren't directly involved, and knew what happened, I wouldn't have believed it. This sort of thing only happens in the movies, but this was real life, my life.

"Stacey, the agents are here." Andrew said after answering the door.

I hadn't realized that he'd moved until I saw him walking towards me. After hitting Ben and I still don't care what anyone says, I don't regret doing it. In my book, he had that coming and more. But because I hit him and other things, Tracey suggested that I go to the doctor. They put me on some medication for anxiety and depression. Which I hate taking because it puts me in such a blah state of mind, and I would rather be alert for my baby.

"Hello, Ms. Johnson. My name is Agent Hill, and this is Agent Collins. We are here to share some information regarding your child, Cameron Lassiter."

"Please have a seat." My mother told them.

"Thank you, ma'am. We know this has been a trying time as it would be for anyone in your situation," Agent Hill said. "But we wanted to let you know where we were so far in the investigation. At this very moment, thanks to the help of Benjamin Harris and the Birmingham City Police Department, we have located the home where your baby is currently being kept. The house is under 24 hour surveillance, and as of ten minutes ago, we observed your baby. He looked to be well taken care of." He said.

"Thank you, Jesus!" Big Mama shouted.

Everyone was celebrating the good news. "So, when will they bring him home?" I asked, trying to express my excitement too, but couldn't.

"We are in the process of developing a plan of extraction. Our goal is to return your child to you safely, therefore this may take some time. We wanted to give this update and ask that you do not share any of this information with anyone outside of this room. We do not want his abductor to know that she is being watched. Our observation and learning about her, revealed that a botched abortion left her infertile. This would further explain her fixation on being a mother. This obsession with your baby is what's keeping him safe. Any premature or unsettling movements can cause that environment to change drastically and we don't want to risk him being harmed."

"I understand," came out of mouth, but that's not how I felt. My feelings said go get my damn baby now!

"Thank you all so much for telling us. We were very worried. This has been a nightmare for his mother and I." Andrew said.

"We'll be sure to keep you all in the loop when more information becomes available. Our purpose today was to inform you all to know that we have found him and are working hard to bring him home to you."

"Thanks again." I said, but didn't mean. This was a bunch of bull. If you can see him, you can get him. He was my baby, not hers. It wasn't my fault that she couldn't have any children take that up with doctors, but give me my child back. I was relieved to hear that he was okay, but fear still loomed over me.

Chapter 11

TAMARA

When I spoke to Ben the other night, I heard a lot of commotion in the background, but couldn't hear what was being said. I thought he would have called me back, but I hadn't heard from anymore since this afternoon. He had asked me out for lunch and I agreed to meet him.

"Hey stranger, " he said, kissing me on the cheek.

"Hey, how are you?" I asked him.

"Busy. You know I'm doing the job of two people."

"I'm sure you are, but remember you were the one that decided to become a one man show."

"Yeah, I know. But now, I'm starting to rethink that great idea, because this is wearing me out. Jeff has helped me out and really showed great initiative when I was overwhelm. I'm thinking about offering him Phillip's role."

"That would be a great idea. He was Phillip's executive assistant for years. It's no surprise to me he's been doing his thing."

"That's a done deal, then. Now, all I have to do is focus on you."

"Focus on me. Why?" I asked.

"Because you're trying to leave me."

"You left me first." I countered.

"Tamara really? I've never left you?"

"What would you call it, then?" I asked.

"Being stupid, immature, and childish."

"I'll accept that."

"It's true." He confessed. "That's like the stupid mess that happened the other day."

"What happened the other day?"

"Stacey." He said.

"What now? When we were hanging up, I heard a bunch of commotion in the background."

"Check this out." He said. "While I was standing there talking to you, Stacey's unhinged ass walks up and slaps the shit out of me. No lie."

"In church? Are you serious!?" I asked.

"Yeah man, talking about how dare you laugh and have a good time while my baby is missing."

"No way." I said in disbelief.

"I'm like, what is your problem? Then, her dude, I guess, felt some kind of way, steps to me talking about don't talk to her that way. Man, please. He better be glad that I didn't slap her ass back."

"Y'all acting like this in the church? I know pop was beside himself."

"Y'all? I was standing there minding my own business, talking to my wife when I got assaulted."

"Give her some grace, Ben. You know she's going through something no parent ever wants to imagine or experience."

"I know one thing, she'll meet His grace if she hits me again."

"I can't with you." I said, laughing. "Thanks for asking me out for lunch. You and your drama." I said, shaking my head.

"You're welcome. I wanted to talk to you about something, anyway."

"Oh, okay, what's up?" I asked, before taking a sip of my sweet tea.

"It's regarding us."

"I'm listening." I said.

"I'm ready to get back to us. I feel like we've spent too much time being apart. I want my wife back. Tamara, I want you to come home. We need to work this out." He admitted.

"Ben, I hear you, but can I be transparent?"

"Absolutely."

"I have made a decision regarding our marriage. I took the time to work through my thoughts and feelings, and Ben, for me, it's not going to work."

"How do you know?" He asked.

"I know me. I know that I will never be able to trust you again."

"What if we go to counseling to sort it all out?"

"We can go to counseling-"

"I was thinking it would help us worked through things." He said, interrupting me.

"And yet, even that wouldn't be enough for me." I told him.

"It's Marcus, isn't it?" He asked annoyed.

"Believe it or not, it isn't. What happened between Marcus and I, puts what occurred between you and me into perspective. I made a whole fool out of myself, thinking that man had wronged me only because I wouldn't hear him out. Then you came along and was like a breath of fresh air. It occurred to me that we both had loose ends that we didn't handle properly, and because we didn't, something horrible happened. We both deserve clean slates, Ben, just not with each other."

"I understand. I don't like it, but I get it."

"I had to do the work. I had to find out what led me to make the decisions that I had, and that required me to be honest with myself."

"So you blame me, too, huh?"

"Not at all, Ben. Can I still be transparent?"

"Sure, go ahead. You have been so far, I guess." He said, a little agitated.

"I can openly admit to still being in love with Marcus. He confronted me about how I felt, but I chose my career over my heart, and married you instead. So no, I can't blame you alone for how things turned out between us."

"Did you all sleep together?"

I was hesitant to answer the question, but I had to be honest with him. "Yes." I whispered.

"Woooow," he said, leaning back in his chair, astonished. "I'm not even believing this. Tamara, did you ever love me?" He asked.

"I did and do, but not like I did him. And in my defense, Ben, before you crash out, I tried to tell you about it after you proposed."

"And I stopped you. I remember." He said dryly.

"Had I told you then, I wonder what would've happened? Would Phillip even be alive today?"

"Possibly, who knows? I know that I was so busy trying to cover up my own dirt, I don't think you telling me what happened between the two of you would change much of anything. I was already deeply in love with you and knew that I didn't want to lose you. But if you had told me that you still loved him, we wouldn't have gotten married."

"Like I told you before, I had to do the work and I was honest with myself. It's your turn to ask yourself what led you to make the decisions that you made? Once you find that out, then you can examine if what you say you want is what you actually need. You'll be shock as I was to learn it doesn't always add up."

"I wasn't expecting lunch to turn out this way, but I thank you for your transparency. Thank you for being honest with me. Now, can I be honest with you?"

"Absolutely." I said.

"I like what I found in you, and I don't want to start over. I think you need to come home with me." He said, smiling. It was as if everything I just said went in one ear and out of the other.

"Something is seriously wrong with you." I said to him.

"I heard you girl, but I'm for real. Relationships are too hard. It's better to stick with what you got and work it out until the other person dies. That's how they did it back in the day. They called it graveyard love. Nobody moved on, they just stuck it out."

"That ain't us. They also cheated on one another too. I'm not trying to live like that."

"What makes you think that will be our fate? Was sleeping with Phillip your way of getting back at me?" He asked.

"Not at all. I just know that I wouldn't want a marriage that I had to question my spouse's every single movement."

"I see. I'm just thinking of our commitment to one another, but you're right, I guess."

"Trust me, everything will be just fine. I have no doubt in my mind that you're going to be okay, I promise."

"You say that now, but what you don't know is that you're about to be stuck with a sidepiece for an ex-husband. I'm telling you right now, so don't go trying to disown me."

"Who raised you? Eat your food so we can get back to work. " I told him.

Ben was not the type to give up on something he wanted easily. For the rest of our lunch, he spent his time discussing how we could make our marriage work. I sat there eating and listening. I had nothing more to add. I had made up my mind, and Ben's persuasion wouldn't change the fact that we were getting a divorce. I allowed him to speak his peace until his heart was content.

Chapter 12

TJ

Since the baby was due at any moment, I had no time to waste. I wanted to propose to Erica before she gave birth to our daughter. I had everything planned out. I told her that I wanted to do something special for her today. That made her smile because she was still upset by the gift she'd received from Kherington. That situation made everything clear to me. I could no longer afford to take life for granted. The thought of someone being able to reach my family was unsettling. Thank God the gift and card were cleared of anything harmful. The Kherington I knew wouldn't dare do anything to hurt anyone, but whoever this new person was didn't care about anything or anybody, and she'd proven it time and time again.

Erica and I just arrived at her favorite restaurant. She was all smiles. My poor baby was going through it. All she complained about was her backaches, being tired, and how much weight she'd gained. But she was beautiful to me and though we've been through a lot these last few months, I wouldn't want to do life with anyone else other than her. She was my rock, like I was hers no matter what.

"Alright beautiful, we're here." I said, parking the car.

"Good, because, I'm hungry."

"Yep, sounds like it's about that time for you two to throw down."

"That's not me, that's the baby that has me eating like this," she said as I helped her out of the car.

"Un-huh, I know it." I agreed quickly. I may act like a fool, but I wasn't one. Disagreeing with her would only have us in a forty-five minute discussion about how I'll never know what it means to be pregnant. I learned that the hard way when I said the toilet paper should be in the over position rather than under. Lawd, why did I say that?

She talked to me for a whole hour, and cried for twenty

minutes, all because I said what I thought. I was all kinds of

insensitive and uncaring obscenities that was until I gave

her a banana moon pie. She became my friend again after

that. Erica had me about ready to give her the Ms. Celie's

fingers. I was about to tell that helfa until she do right by

me, every student she taught was gon fail. I was sick of her

mistreating me, but that was my baby.

I requested for a table in the back for more privacy.

It was one of her favorite places because it was a nice low

key spot that had dimmed lights and offered soft music that

played in the background. After placing our orders, Erica

had to go back to the bathroom. Which was cool because it

gave me enough time to practice what I was going to say to

her when she returned. I placed the ring in the middle of

her saucer and placed the saucer in front of her chair as I

anxiously waited. It was taking her longer than usual,

which meant she saw someone she knew coming back from

the bathroom. Finally, I thought when I saw her walking back to our table.

"Is everything okay?" I asked, holding out her chair.

"Oh my God!" She shouted as she sat down.

"Baby," I said kneeling next to her. "You have been with me when I was at my lowest and you've helped me to become the man that I am today. I love you with everything that I am and want you to be my wife. Will you marry me?"

"Oh, my God, oh my God!"

"Is that a yes, baby?" I asked, all excited.

"Uggghhh."

"Ugh? What the hell does that mean?" I asked, confused.

"That means my water just broke and I'm in labor, fool!" She said, practicing the breathing that we learned in Lamaze class.

I slid the ring on her finger and rushed her to the hospital as fast as my SUV would carry us while thanking God that I had leather seats.

After arriving at the hospital, they got her registered and placed in a room quickly. I don't know who was more nervous, her or me. This was not my first rodeo, but it was just as scary. Especially hearing about all the things that could go wrong during labor and delivery with women of color. I believed this worried Erica the most. Every time she came across a story online, she shared it with me. My heart went out to all those women that lost their lives, sometimes along with their babies. Often, I was at a loss for words because how could I reassure her that the same wouldn't happen to us? It may have been over the top for most women, but Erica joined a support group to discuss her fears. The support group taught us the warning signs to look out for during labor and post delivery. They helped her to maintain a healthy weight by focusing on nutrition factors that not only would support the baby, but her as well. So far, she had done well and her physician was encouraging her to push. Soon, we will be welcoming a healthy baby girl.

Chapter 13

TAMARA

It was three in the morning when Ben called to tell me that Erica was in labor. I jumped up and dressed so fast that I wasn't sure if my shoes even matched. After arriving at the hospital, I found Ben, who was already waiting in the lobby.

"Good morning," he said, kissing me on the cheek.

"Morning. How is she doing? Have you heard anything yet?" I asked him.

"Nothing yet. I arrived about twenty minutes before you did, but I text TJ to let him know that I was here. I see you were in a hurry to get here." He said, laughing.

I looked down at my feet and saw that my shoes matched. "Why do you say that?" I asked.

"I've never seen you in a hair bonnet before."

Sure enough, I rushed out of the house in my hair bonnet. "I have to keep some things about myself a mystery." I said after taking the bonnet off.

"Bonnet on or off. You'll always be sexy to me, Mrs. Harris."

"Whatever." I said, trying to stop blushing.

"Hey guys," TJ said. "Thank y'all for coming."

"Now you know we were coming." Ben responded. "Where else would we be?"

"How's my sister doing?" I asked, concerned.

"Come and see for yourselves and meet your niece, A'ja. She's so beautiful." He said.

We followed TJ to Erica's room, where she was holding her precious baby. You could see love all over her, so much so that she glowed.

"Hey mommy," I whispered and hugged her shoulders. "I'm so proud of you." I told her through my tears.

"Say hello baby A'ja to your auntie Tam."

"She's so beautiful." I said, adoring her.

"Thank you." TJ said. "I do make beautiful babies, if I may say so myself."

All we could do was laugh at that nut.

"Congratulations Sis." Ben said, kissing her on the cheek. "It's time to get those shotguns ready, bro." He told TJ as he held the baby's hand.

"When they told us that she was having a girl, I started buying bullets then."

"You get the day shift and I'll take the night." Ben said.

"She's not even three hours old yet, and she's already on lockdown. Men. Don't worry buttercup, TT has your back" I told the baby.

"Have you called Ce yet?" Ben asked.

"Nah, because of the time. I just hit the ones she would want to let know. I'll call everyone else later this morning, or send a post to the baby's page online." He said.

"That'll be good. I know she needs her rest." Ben said.

"Me and Ma Dukes will be here with them."

"Where is she?" I asked.

"She went to the cafeteria to find some coffee and snacks."

"TJ, can you come and place her in the bassinet for me?" Erica asked.

"Are you getting sleepy?" I asked her as I readjusted the covers.

"I am. The adrenaline is wearing off and the pain meds are kicking in."

"Is that what I think it is?" I said, looking at her left hand.

"Oh yeah, I proposed last night." TJ said proudly.

"That's what's up!" Ben said, dapping him up.

"Congratulations boo." I said, gently hugging her.

"That's not all," TJ said. "We would like for the two of you to be our baby's godparents."

"When we talked about it, you two were all that came to mind," Erica said.

Ben and I exchanged looks.

"What's wrong?" Erica asked me.

"Yeah bro, what was that look for?" TJ asked.

"How can we say this, umm." I said.

"We're divorcing." Ben finished for me.

"What tha hell? Ah man." TJ said, sitting down.

"Listen, guys. We know it comes to everyone as a shock, but this was a mutual decision that we made together." Ben said, while holding my hand.

"And we will continue to be the best of friends." I said, smiling at him.

"I told her that I would be her sidepiece." Ben said.

"Only you would say some mess like that," Erica said, laughing. "But seriously, I hate it came to this. I really do, but I understand."

"Yeah, me too, bro. I hate to hear this, man. Have y'all told the folks? They are going to be devastated."

"I know. My mom doesn't know anything. This was something we just recently made a decision on, and I haven't had the heart to tell her about anything that has happened with us, or Phillip's passing. I know she's going to have a lot of questions." I said.

"Ms. Cookie is going to flip when she hears about everything." Erica said.

"I know. I'm still not ready to tell her." I said.

"Same here, me either with my parents. You're the first to know. To be honest, this is the first time the words have come out of my mouth." Ben said, hopelessly.

"Okay guys, let's change the subject. We're here to celebrate you all, and to welcome baby A'ja. If it's okay with you all, I'd still love to be this sweet girl's

godmother." I said rubbing her back as she slept.

"Same here, bro. I would be honored to be her

godfather."

"Our opinions about y'all ain't changed. We're

shocked, maybe, but nothing has changed. Right babe?" TJ

asked Erica.

"Right." She agreed.

"I can't wait to start planning this fabulous

wedding, girl." I said to Erica.

"First things first. Let me shed this baby weight and

it's on."

"As maid of honor, just put me in something fitting

and sexy. She'll be single and ready to mingle." I said,

laughing.

"Too soon Mrs. Harris, too soon." Ben said,

frowning.

"Anyway, girl," I said rolling my eyes at him. "I'm about to get out of here so that you can get some rest. Tell mama to call me if you all need anything."

"I will." She said, yawning.

"Alright bro, I'm heading out, too. I'll check on you guys later on. Kiss the baby goodbye for me."

"Congratulations again, you two. I love y'all and will see you later." I said as Ben and I walked out the door together.

"Can I take you to breakfast?" Ben asked while we waited on the elevator to arrive.

"Sure. What's open this early in the morning?"

He smiles, "Our house." He said.

"Ben, I'm going to go back to where I live and get back in my bed. I'm not playing with you."

"I'm so serious. No funny business. I promise." He said, laughing.

"You promise?"

"I promise. Let me cook you breakfast this last time as Mrs. Harris." He said, seriously.

"I'm down, but if you do anything, I'm out of there. Let's go." I told him.

"I hope that you don't have anything planned until this afternoon because this is about to be the longest, slowest cooked breakfast you ever had in your life."

All I could do was shake my head and laugh at him. Ben had something up his sleeve, but I'm not falling for it. "I will not be seduced." I told myself aloud as I followed him home. The slightest feeling of discomfort and I'm out of there. I know him well and he doesn't play fair. If I let him have his way, I'd be naked before the toast to could pop up. "Nope, I will not be seduced." I said as I pulled into the garage and watching him get out of his car.

Chapter 14

BENJAMIN

I should've thought about doing this months ago. Tamara could never resist my breakfast. I cooked all of her favorites too. There was no way that we would eat all this food, but I'll do just about anything to keep her here with me. I had my music playing and the mimosas pouring. We were vibing and having a great time.

"Come on, let's dance this breakfast off." Eric Roberson's song *Lessons* allowed me to bring her body close to mine. At that moment, I never wanted to forget how she felt in my arms. I never wanted to forget how our rhythm was always in sync. I desperately needed to remember her fragrance. I wanted to freeze this moment in time. I wished I could express my heart to her so she would receive and understand it. I wished forgiveness between us was simple as saying, I'm sorry. For now, this was all I had to hold on to, and unfortunately for me, it would have to last me a lifetime.

She held me as tight as I held her. I wondered what she was thinking. The next song played, and we kept slow dancing. Not a word spoken. When I stepped back to twirl her around, that's when I saw her face was full of tears.

"Tamara, I-" She placed her finger up to my lips.

"I'm okay. Let's just dance." She whispered.

I held her closer to me without moving. At that time, I realized what she was doing. She was saying goodbye to us. She was letting go, and because she was letting go of me, I had to do the same for her. I've never known a loss like this. It ripped my heart to shreds to love her so much, and know this was the end of us. Letting her go would be the hardest thing I'd ever have to do. I had lost the greatest love I'd ever known and there was nothing I could do about it but cry, and we did so together.

***

I received a phone call from Detective Bennett about the case. He wanted to give me an update.

"Hello Mr. Harris. How's it going today?"

"I can't lie, detective. I've seen better days."

"I think I have some news that may cheer you up?"

"Oh yeah, what's that?" If it wasn't Tamara has changed her mind, then what could it be?

"It's been confirmed that the FBI has eyes on Kherington and they are getting a plan in motion to rescue the baby and arrest her. I knew it was only a matter of time before she slipped up, and using that card was her first and final mistake."

"I can't believe that this nightmare is almost over." I told him.

"Yes sir. Has she tried to contact you again?"

"No, she hasn't. I've tried calling the number she called me from and all it does is ring."

"Well, if she calls again, let us know immediately. I know the FBI has taken over the case, but they'd be interested in knowing this information. She may reach out to you again. I can't imagine her being isolated for long."

"I will let you know whenever she does. Thanks again."

"You're welcome. Take care." He said.

Chapter 15

KHERINGTON

This is the first day in a while that my head didn't feel like it was being split into. I saw where Ben had been calling me, but I couldn't answer. Hopefully, he's not upset with me because his family needs him. The baby has been a complete angel. He only cries when he's wet, and for that I am thankful. Our little sweetpea is such a happy baby, all he does is coos and smiles. I saw on Facebook that Erica had her baby and she is a gorgeous little something. I hope that she enjoys the gift that I sent her. Maybe one day they can come and visit us so that our two kids can get to know one another.

I put the baby in his bed and called Ben.

"Kherington!" He shouted.

"Hey baby. Sorry, it took me a while to call you back. I haven't been feeling so well, but I'm feeling much better now."

"You've been sick?" He asked.

"I have these really bad headaches sometimes."

"How are you caring for Cameron?"

"Now what kind of mother would I be if I didn't take care of our son despite these stupid headaches?"

"Our son?"

"Yes, silly." I said. "Where is your mind?"

"You're right. Where's our son at now?" He asked.

"He's in his bed waiting for his daddy to come home."

"I'm ready to come home too, baby. But I don't know where you and the baby are."

"I know you don't, silly. No one does." I said, laughing.

"Well, how am I supposed to see you and baby? I miss you, sweetheart, and I want to see my son. I haven't seen my little man since he was born. Do you think you could send me a pic of him, and of course, you too? Maybe even together?"

"Ah, I miss you too, babe. Sure I can."

"So, what are you going to do about it?" He said, sounding sexy.

"Ooh, don't say that like that to me. Do you know how sexy you sound?" He was turning me on.

"Baby, I really need to see you. Don't you love me?"

"Very much."

"Well, send me the address to your location so that I can pull up on you, and don't forget the pics."

"I will, but what about Tamara?" I asked him.

"What about her?" He asked.

"Do you still want to be with her?"

"No. I'm leaving her for you. I'm divorcing her. I'm so in love with you, Kherington. You are all I can think about."

"I am! I knew we should've been together. Phillip keeps telling me you didn't love me."

"Phillip does what?"

"Yeah, don't worry. I don't believe a word that comes out of his lying mouth. I just ignore him. I knew you loved me."

"You're right not to listen." He said slowly.

"Well, I'm going to send you pictures and the address when I want you to come, okay? Bye." I said before hanging up. My headache was starting to pound and Phillip was watching me like a hawk. He's been on my case ever since I almost dropped Cameron in the tub when I was giving him a bath. The book didn't tell me how slippery babies could be when they're soapy and wet. I caught him before he hit the water. Shoot. All this time Phillip has had nothing to say. That incident happened and now I can't shut

him up. If he wants to be helpful, do something about these

stupid non-stop headaches, and takeout the garbage

sometime. He talks to me more now than the entire time we

dated. I never knew how annoying he was. It made me

wonder if he was this way with Tamara.

Chapter 16

BENJAMIN

"Damn it!" I almost had the address.

"Who are you talking to, bro?" TJ asked, walking into the house.

"Kherington." I said, frustrated.

"You talked to her? What did she say? Where is she?" He asked frantically.

"That's the thing. I was trying to get her to give me the address to where she was."

"I can't believe you actually talked to her. Have you called the police?"

"No, and please don't tell anyone else."

"Why not?" He asked, confused. "Listen, man. We have to let the police know right away."

"According to them, they already have eyes on her."

"Well, how come they haven't arrested her yet?" He asked.

"That's what I wanted to know. But for now, I'm going to do whatever I can to help move the process along."

"How are you-"

"Hold up. She just sent me a video." I said, cutting him off.

"Hey baby, here we are mommy and son." She said. I was taken aback by how awful she looked. She had dark circles under her sunken eyes. She looked to have lost about twenty pounds. "He's getting so big, isn't he?" Kherington said, smiling in the camera.

"What tha hell?" TJ asked. He was just as stunned as I was.

"Will you shut the hell up, damn? See what I'm talking about, babe? That's all he does is run off at the mouth. You act like this is your son." She said, talking to no one.

"Who is she talking to?" TJ asked as we continued to watch the video in shock and horror.

"Phillip."

"Say who now?" He asked. "He's dead. She killed him."

"Yes, I know."

"Well, how is she talking to somebody that's already dead?" He asked.

"She's lost it, man. That's why I gotta find them."

"Babe, do you think he impregnated our surrogate?" She asked, looking at the camera. "Let me see. Our baby is too yellow to be his, anyway." She said, looking Cameron over. "Fine. Fine, tell him then. Here he is. Tell him!" She said, flipping the camera to an empty corner of the room. Not a word heard.

"This is straight up crazy, man. Like for real. The police needs to know about this." TJ said.

"Are you satisfied now, damn? Just get on my nerves. He didn't need to know all of that." She said in a full argument before the video ended.

"I didn't need to know what?!" I shouted at my phone.

"Oh, my God. Kherington has really lost her mind." TJ said.

"Cameron is in far greater danger than anyone knows." I said, trying to call her back, but like the last time, the phone just rung. **"Damn it!"** I shouted.

"But you said the police said they had eyes on her."

"Yeah, but they haven't arrested her yet. I need to find her before she does something to that baby."

"I understand because I'll go to war for mine, but he is not yours Ben, so why not let the police handle it?

"Because I feel responsible for this. No, I didn't tell her to kill Phillip, kidnap the baby, or anything else she may have done, but because of me, she did."

"And for that reason, you definitely need to let the police handle it. She has killed once. Don't you know she'll do it again?"

"That's a chance I have to take. The baby is in serious trouble. You saw that for yourself." I told him.

"Bro, did you see how demented she was? I've never seen anyone look like that before." He said.

"I'm just thankful that the baby looked well taken care of. He looked happy, didn't he?"

"Yeah, he did, but considering who his mammy is, he probably feels right at home with Kherington. I still don't agree with you wanting to be a vigilante." TJ said.

"I gotta track her down." I said, while looking at the purchases.

"Since you are clearly not listening to me, how can I help?" He asked.

"I need to find out where these packages are going?" I said.

"These are all Amazon transactions. You know they send a confirmation email of the order being sent."

"Yeah, but how would I know the email address that it's being sent to?" I asked.

"How are you seeing these transactions?"

"She's been using Phillip's credit card."

"Damn, I guess since she killed him, she thought it would be okay to take over his identity, too. If she's using his card, maybe she's using his business Amazon account too. Are you able to see his H & G emails?"

"Yep, let's see. Here they are?"

"Okay, the email should tell you where they are being shipped to." TJ said.

"I wonder what would happen if I pressed view or manage order?" I said out loud. Finally, I was able to find her location. "But this says the items are being delivered to a locker at CVS."

"That means where ever this is, she's not too far from it. Let's see where this CVS is?" He said.

Two heads were always better than one. We found the location of where she was hiding. Now all I needed to do was to convince her to meet me with the baby.

***

Two days later, Kherington called me back and agreed to meet me with Cameron. I broke all kinds of traffic laws to get to the McDonald's off of W Fort Williams Street in Sylacauga. I arrived early. I sat there and thought about how I was going to get Cameron from her. I even had a baby car seat in the back seat of my car. After watching several Youtube channels on how to install the thing, I was able to secure the seat in place. This was how hopeful I was of getting him back.

Man, where is she? I kept looking at the clock and watched everyone that pulled up next to me. Twenty minutes had passed, and no Kherington. By this time I was pissed off, and I called the last number she had called me from.

"Hello." She answered.

"Where are you? You have me out here looking crazy waiting for you."

"I'm sorry, baby, but we're not going to be able to come today."

"Why not? I drove all this way to-"

"Because something isn't right." She said, cutting me off.

"What do you mean, something isn't right?"

"Like I said, something isn't right. The vibe is all off. We have to make it for another time, okay?"

"Kherington, I really need to see you and my son. Can I just come to you all and-"

"No," she replied, cutting me off. "It'll be too dangerous."

"So you don't love me anymore, I see." I said, trying to get into her head.

"You know I do. I just can't risk our baby being taken from us. His surrogate mother is trying to claim him as hers. Did you know about that?"

"Um, no. But how do you know about it?" I lied.

"I've seen her on TV crying. She can't have our baby. I won't stand for it! She's telling lies to them about me. I may have to pay her a visit to put a stop to the lies she's been telling."

"No! Please, don't do that. She's not worth it. You're right, keep our baby safe." I urged her.

"I'll call you back as soon as I can. Bye." She said before hanging up.

From my rearview window, I saw two black and white patrol cars and another unmarked car was in the same parking lot just spaces down from me. I don't know how she knew it, but she was right. They found out and somehow followed me here. Damn it! I called Detective Bennett immediately.

"Detective Bennett." He answered.

"This is Benjamin Harris."

"Mr. Harris, what can I do for you?"

"Explain to me why in the hell I'm being followed?"

"I think that would be a better question for the FBI. Just a moment."

"Agent Collins." He said.

"Uh, I have Mr. Harris on the line and I'm going to connect you with him."

"Thanks." The agent said. "Mr. Harris?"

"Yes."

"How may I help you?"

"Can someone tell me what is going on, and why am I being followed?"

"Can you tell me why you're in Sylacauga?" He asked.

"I'm here to meet someone."

"And would that someone happened to be Kherington Draker?"

"I was. She called me and all I wanted to do was get the baby back."

"Sounds like to me that you are helping her."

"Not at all. I wanted to get the baby from her. You don't understand."

"All you were going to do was interfere with our investigation. You should have called us immediately when she contacted you. You do know that you can be arrested and charged as an accomplice, right?"

"All I know is that I would have been successful at my attempt had you all not spooked her away. Now she may never come out of hiding, or believe me, for that matter. I need to get the baby away from her. She is very unstable, and it's only a matter of time before she loses control and possibly does something to the baby." I said, angrily.

"And you would know this how?"

"She sent me a video of her and the baby. Cameron appears to be well taken care of, but what disturbed me the most is what she does in the video."

"And that would be?"

"She is arguing with my deceased business partner. Apparently, he talks to her and only she can see and hear him."

"I see. So from what you are explaining is that she is suffering from bouts of schizophrenia?"

"I don't know the medical terminology. All I can say is Cameron is in great danger, and today may have made her more paranoid." I told him.

"I understand the severity of the case and your desire to want to help, but you must allow us to do what we do. You are right in saying the child is in great danger, but we can't afford to have any interferences."

"I know I can reach her and I can get Cameron back. Please let me help you. She trusts me, but you all will need to give me time and space to do it."

"I don't know. I will have to talk to my team about this."

"That's all I'm asking, please." I said, hoping to have pleaded my case.

"I'll discuss this with my team and get back to you."

"Thank you."

"Sure. For now, please do not act on your own."

"I understand." I said before hanging up. Everyone says they understand, but no one is acting on anything. At least I tried.

Chapter 17

TAMARA

I'll be the first to admit that things had become strained between Ben and me after discussing our divorce. I spoke with him last night to confirm my coming to the house to remove the rest of my things. He informed me then that Kherington was no longer a threat to us. I was so relieved to hear that. No more security. No more watching over my shoulder. I wanted to know more details, but he seemed distracted. Whatever he had going on was more important than my concern because when I tried to press him for more information, he became short with me and said in so many words that he couldn't provide any further details, and hung-up.

My new normal has finally arrived, I thought as I looked around the room to see if I was leaving anything behind. To think I was packing up my belongings to move was almost inconceivable. In arrogance, I sold my townhouse and furnishings, thinking I would never have a need for them. Look at me now. I had more boxes now than I did before moving into Ben's house. The only thing I brought with me were my clothes and shoes. I depended on him to provide everything else, and for the most part, he had. Everything was in the truck except for this last box.

Just when I thought that my life had fallen completely apart, I received what I needed the most to put it back together again. I got closure. As heartbreaking and tragic as it was, I needed a fresh new start. I never thought that I'd find myself divorced. That's not the life that I chose for myself. I wanted to be happy and in love. But as life would have it and I've come to learn, you can't fix the unbroken. Meaning, if I stayed in the delusion of everything will be okay without dealing with what broke me to begin with, I'd never heal. This is what happened between Marcus and me. I refused to deal with what hurt me, and because of that, I didn't allow one door to close before opening another.

I was honest with Ben when I told him about my choices. That didn't mean that I hadn't loved him because I did. Even now, I loved Ben and heard everything he had to say. But the reality of it all for me was not being in love with him anymore. The facade of him being a faithful husband had been destroyed beyond repair. He could no longer pull the wool over my eyes. Someone would think that I was being over the top, but I wasn't. I know that it may seem unfair of how I treated him. His actions made it easy for me to change. After making one mistake there should be forgiveness, and there was, but that didn't mean I could ever trust him again. And I know from Ben's point of view I may come off as a hypocrite, and maybe I was, but all I knew was too much had happened between us to be together. The broken trust between us could never be resealed. Unlike Marcus, I caught Ben in the act. I had no other choice but to deal with what had occurred. It was right there in my face. And this time, I didn't have to assume a single thing. I had proof.

At the end of the day, Ben and I were both wrong. He cheated, and I cheated, but for different reasons. None of them good reasons that could be justified. His reasons are his reasons, and I may never learn why. I just know things would never be the same. My heart still flutters whenever I see him, and perhaps it always will. I just know not to act on those feelings. Feelings had me where I was today, divorced.

For this reason separation from him was necessary. I've had plenty of time to think and rethink about our marriage and the man I thought I knew doesn't exist. As charming and handsome as he was, I really wondered what made Ben want to get married. It's not like he couldn't have any woman that he wanted, so why settle down? It's almost as if he likes the thrill of the chase, and when the tables turn, he cannot resist. So, if we stayed married, what's to stop him from ending up in the bed of the next woman? Absolutely nothing. This man was used to getting any and everything that he wanted whenever he wanted, and nothing was going to stop him from doing so now.

Did I believe he loved me, yes I did. But not enough to deny himself of the temptation of another woman.

"Hey, I see you're just about finished in here." He said, watching me place the last of my things in a box.

"Yep, I'm just about finished."

"I'm going to miss you." He said.

"I know, but you'll be seeing me around, I'm sure." I said nonchalantly.

"Tamara, really?" He asked, touching my arm.

"Ben, I don't know what else to say at this point."

"Say that you don't want to go and call this stupid divorce off."

"But I can't and you know that. We've talked about this." I told him.

"All I know is that I love you."

"I love you too, but things aren't the same anymore."

"But they can be if you allow them to. What happened to for better or for worse?"

"If I allowed them to, Ben? Okay, what's to stop you from being tempted and cheating again?"

"I'm what's stopping me. Listen, I can admit that I was wrong. I was wrong to lie about Stacey. I was wrong for sleeping with Kherington. I was wrong for asking you to join my company to prevent you from learning the truth about me and Stacey. I was wrong for a lot of things, but one thing I'll never be sorry for doing is asking you to be my wife. I meant every single word that I vowed to you on our wedding day."

"Every word except forsaking all others." I countered.

"Okay, you're right. I didn't honor you as I should have. I take accountability for that, but what about you?"

"What about me?" I snapped back.

"Where was your accountability when you slept with Phillip? I even shouldered that. I blamed it on me, but at the end of the day, it was you who also chose to dishonor your wedding vows. Yes, I am a man that fell into temptation of another. Yes, I did that, but at least I can face the actions of my choices and not run away from them. Can you be woman enough to do the same?" He asked, before leaving me alone in our bedroom. I couldn't believe he spoke to me that way.

I gathered the last of my things and placed the full box near the door that led to the garage. Without another word spoken to him, I took my wedding rings off along with the keys to his house and placed them both on the kitchen counter before picking up the rest of my belongings

to leave. I exited his house, knowing that would be the last

time that I'd see or speak to him again. As I slowly pulled

out of the garage, looking in the rearview mirror, I saw Ben

standing there watching me leave as the garage door slowly

closed behind me.

Chapter 18

MARCUS

A few weeks ago, Tamara took my SUV to go and

pick up the rest of her things. She placed a few of her boxes

in my garage until she decided where she wanted to move. I

talked her into continuing to stay with me for obvious

reasons. I have enjoyed every moment spent with her. I

noticed when she returned from gathering her things that

she had become a bit down. I learned on their last

encounter that there was a mix of words between them that

unsettled her. She didn't like that he called her a runner. I

was there to listen and not to judge, but if I was to judge,

I'd agree with him. I know Tamara didn't see herself in this

way, but what he said was the truth. She will defend

herself, but to deal with confrontation, nope, she's out of

there. Tamara was not the type to wait around and see. I

love her dearly, but she was not. Call me petty. I did,

however, point out that had she not run away from me, she'd never known life with Benjamin. I'm was just telling the truth. She was getting ready to argue her point of view, but became quiet and conceded.

I just knew for sure that she was going to call Public Storage and rent a small U-Haul after that, but she didn't. Somehow, things just clicked, and her mood changed. I didn't press her about what was going on in her head because if she had wanted me to know, she would've shared her thoughts with me. Between the two of us, we always had open, honest communication that I appreciated. There was no guessing with her, and I loved that we were still that way even today.

I gave her space when she and Benjamin signed their divorce papers. She said their attorneys had never witnessed such an amicable divorce. She didn't take anything from him and he didn't take anything from her, not even the cars they had purchased for each other for

Christmas. No one contested anything, they had no reason to. She told me that it would be a month or so before being finalized. I still gave her space. She came to me and asked why I was being so distant from her. I told her sometimes people change their minds. She told me she understood but her mind about her marriage had been made up. According to her, she was settled and content. Where have I heard that before? In my opinion, I felt like Tamara was still very much in love with Benjamin, just hurt. We haven't discussed how she felt that's just my observation. All I know is until she deals with whatever it was that she's trying to suppress, she will always wrestle back and forth with her emotions.

As her friend, I wanted to do something nice for her. It had been a while since we'd been out. I took her to a spot that we used to go to when we first started dating, J. Alexander's, in Hoover.

"No, you didn't! I haven't been here in so long."
She said, shocked.

"I just wanted to do something nice for you."

"Aww, you're so sweet."

"I try." I said before getting out to open her car
door.

"I already know what I want to eat too." She said as
I held the door open to go inside. "How did you remember
that this was one of my favorite places?"

"Girl, there's not too much that I don't remember
about you."

"Stop it. You're about to make me blush." She said,
smiling.

"It's true. But you already know how I feel, so I
won't rehash anything."

"I do, but it's always good to hear how you feel."
She said, smiling

"Girl, let me find out you feeling your boy." I teased her. "Well, how about this? Let's enjoy our meal and time together, and I'll share my thoughts with you later on. How about that?" I asked.

"That sounds good to me." She said.

We ate our dinner and enjoyed the ambience of the restaurant. The food was good as always and the steaks simply melted in our mouths. We continued to talk as I drove us home on full stomachs.

"Thank you. I needed that." She said.

"It was my pleasure. I'm glad you enjoyed yourself."

"I did. This is me getting back to being me."

"Oh yeah," I said, laughing.

"I can stop looking over my shoulder and jumping at every sound that I hear."

"It's been a few intense months. I can't lie. I was worried for a moment. Thank God Benjamin had the great idea of hiring security for you all."

"Yeah, that was nice of him, but it was you that saved me." She said as her voice trailed off.

"What's wrong?" I asked as I pulled into the garage.

"It's nothing." She responded quickly.

"Tamara, it's me, remember?"

"I promise." She said shyly.

"Come on, let's go inside. Go get comfortable and I'll meet you back here in the living room."

I sat next to Tamara on the sofa and in my hands were a bottle of Electra wine and two wineglasses.

"Okay, Dr. Worthington, I see you with my favorite wine and everything."

"You know it. Tonight is special."

"What are we celebrating?"

"You."

"Me? Why?"

"For getting your life back."

"I almost lost it trying to prove myself right."

"But you didn't, and that's worth celebrating."

"I'll cut a rug once I get that phone call that says she's locked up behind bars." She said.

"You and I both. But the good news is that they have eyes on her, and it's only a matter of time before she's apprehended."

"Cheers to that." She said as we clinked glasses.

"So what was that sadness about earlier?" I asked.

"It's not at all what you're thinking. I mean, the whole thing is just sad. I've lost a good friend and a marriage over what, sex? It's so hard to believe at times."

"I get what you're saying, but listen, you can't blame yourself for walking away and choosing you. Everyone had a role to play, but Kherington was playing a totally different game. She was playing for keeps."

"If I had known she'd wanted Ben that bad, I'd gladly gave him to her if it meant saving the life of my friend."

"That's the thing. You're speaking as if she would've wanted to make that trade, because she had no interest in that. Her goal was to remove both you and Phillip. You two posed a great threat to her happily ever after with Benjamin."

"The joke is on her because he's a free man now, and he wouldn't want her if his life depended on it." She said.

"And that's what makes everything so dangerous for the baby. As long as she believes Benjamin wants a family with her, the baby will remain safe, but as soon as she thinks otherwise, the baby is expendable." I told her.

"Do you think that she would really hurt him?" She asked.

"Didn't she murder Phillip and attempted to do the same to you?" I asked. "Don't get me wrong, I'm not trying to bring down the mood, but you understand what I'm saying. This woman studied your past to find me in order to connect back to you. She is dangerous."

"I've been trying to figure out how, and why you of all people?"

"I thought about that too. I think I have an idea, though."

"What's that?"

"Are you friends with her on social media?"

Tamara gasped, "Yes, we are."

"And you and I are friends on social media."

"Yeah, but I deleted all of my pictures with you when Ben and I got engaged."

"Yeah, but I didn't and my Facebook page is set to public. She had gone through your friend's list and checked out every profile until she came across mine and possibly saw pictures of you and I together."

"But that didn't mean you and I would connect again."

"It would if someone sent me there to meet you. I received a text from what I thought was from a group of doctors I work with asking everyone to meet up at the coffee shop, so I did. Only to bump into you. So the next day when I went to work, and I asked them about the message, no one had a clue of what I was talking about. I showed them the message from my phone, and when they looked at theirs, I was the only recipient."

"Are you serious? How?"

"We still don't know." I said.

"But how would she know that I was at the coffee shop?" She asked.

"The investigator!" We said at the same time.

"Now you understand?"

"I understand. Danger still lurks, and it has an innocent baby she has in her clutches." She said before taking a sip of her wine.

"That's enough talk about them. Tell me about the places you've found to stay, because I know you've been looking?" I said, refilling her wineglass.

"Oh, now you're ready to kick me out, huh?"

"Now you know you can stay here as long as you need."

"Yeah, I know. I just can't thank you enough, Marcus. You've done so much for me, and didn't have to."

"You don't have to thank me."

"But I do. You had my back, and if you had not come into the coffee shop that day, where would I be?" She asked.

That's when I rediscovered again what I believed to be lost to me. I found her heart. Her true feelings had been hidden from me all this time. It was more than gratitude.

This was love. I've been waiting for this moment ever since she walked back into my life. She's all I ever wanted, and now she was finally here.

Chapter 19

TAMARA

Marcus was being modest, but he had saved my life twice. Once from Kherington, and then from myself. He gave me the space I needed to make clear, sound decisions. He had not pressured me in any way. I wasn't blind. I could see that he was still in love with me. It was all in the way he looked at me. His love was nurturing. He cared for me as if I was his prize possession.

"I can't speak about then, but I can tell you all about right now. You should have been by my side where you were always meant to be." He said before kissing me.

And with the same passion, I returned his kisses that left me breathless.

"Are you sure?" He asked.

How could I not be? I thought. I wanted to answer but couldn't form the words. I simply nodded my head yes.

That was all he needed to lift me up from the sofa and into his arms to carry me to his bedroom. He treated my body like it was made of honey-sweet and sticky. Kissing every place he'd missed until I couldn't possibly take it anymore. I was on fire for this man and he knew it. Once he crossed the threshold of my love, I quivered under the weight of him, causing me to reach peaks of pleasure I'd never known. I gave as good as I got round for round, pound for pound. Our passionate lovemaking filled the night with moans and groans until we both collapsed from exhaustion.

I arouse the next morning to the smell of fresh brewed coffee and bacon. I hopped out of bed and went into his bathroom to take a shower. I dried off and found one of his t-shirts in the drawer to wear until I went to my room to dress.

"Good morning." I said, joining him in the kitchen where he had just finished making breakfast.

"Look at you. Ain't nothing like a night of good love making to put a smile on your face like that." He said, kissing me sweetly.

"I can't stand you sometimes." I said, laughing at him.

"I bet. How are you feeling this morning? I thought I was going to have to come in there and wake you up."

"I feel wonderful." I said, smiling. I needed that release.

"No baby, how do you feel about last night, us?"

"I feel good about it."

"So, if I asked you to give us another chance, would you?" He said, fixing our plates.

"I would." I said, following him to the dining room table with our coffee.

"You would?" He turned around and asked.

"Yes, I would." I confirmed.

"Tamara, you're such an amazing woman and I love you so much." He said, placing our plates on the table. "I promise that I will never hurt you again. I promised myself that if I had ever got the chance to get you back that I'd never let you go. Tamara Reed will you do me the honor of becoming my wife?" He asked on bended knee with the most beautiful ring.

***

I was so blindsided by Marcus's proposal that it left me speechless. There was only one person I cared to discuss this with and I was knocking on her front door to tell her all about it.

"Hey Mom. Where's Erica and the baby?" I spoke to Erica's mother after she opened the door and giving her a hug.

"She's upstairs with the baby, laying her down for a nap. How you been?"

"I've been good. How about you? Are you enjoying your grandbaby?"

"Yeah, she's so cute. She reminds me so much of Erica when she was that small. But things are about to get better now that that crazy lady is about to be caught. Umph, all I can do now is watch the news and pray."

"Me too, mom. She has caused enough heartache and trouble I know that much." I said.

"Tam, is that you?" Erica shouted from upstairs.

"Gone go upstairs. She's been waiting for you. We'll talk more when you come back down." Her mother said.

"Yes, ma'am." I said heading for the steps.

"Well hello. Aren't we're all a glow today?" Erica asked, smiling.

"Hello to you, too." I said, hugging her after she place the baby in her bassinet.

"Uh-uh, something's up." She said, looking me up and down. "Why are you glowing like that?" Erica asked being suspicious.

"Girrrrlllll." I said in a low voice. "I came over to spill this tea. It's percolating hot."

"I know it's got to be good. Spill it, spill it. Hold up, don't say a word. Come on, let's get out of here and let my baby sleep. I don't want to miss a spit of this piping hot tea." She said as I followed her into another room. "So what's up?"

"Guess who got together last night?"

"Who?"

"Me and Marcus."

"Helfa, I know you lying!" She shouted.

"Shhhhh." I said, remembering that the baby was asleep in the other room. "No ma'am. And he proposed this morning."

She was getting ready to scream, but covered her mouth instead. "Girl. Shut-up, what!? Oh, my God. What did you say?" She asked excitedly.

"I said yes," I said, tipping my hand so that she could see my beautiful ring.

"Oh, my God! Congratulations sis! It's gorgeous!"

"Thank you, bestie! Girl, I got it right this time." I told her.

"I knew once you went to stay with him that y'all was going to get back together. I just knew it. I was so sure of it, that I bet TJ on it. I can't wait to tell him to cough up my money."

"Y'all are over here betting on my love life?" I asked. "Y'all are pitiful."

"It was really TJ that said I bet she don't. I just came up with the dollar amount. But how do you feel about everything? Hold on. When did he get this ring, and how did he know you would say yes to him?" She asked.

"I asked the same thing. He said it was always his intent to propose, but we had broken up before he could. So he just held onto it in hopes of the day, he'd get the chance to do so."

"That so romantic and sweet."

"I know. To be honest with you, I feel relieved. I feel amazing. I feel loved. That's the best way I can describe how I feel. Girl when I tell you that I wasn't expecting him to do that. Erica, I was so shocked. All I could do was bawl my eyes out. I was so overjoyed. Because I was thinking days before about how I missed out on a good man, and just when I thought good friends were all we were ever going to be, this happened." I said, looking at my ring. "He and I talked about the engagement, amongst other things. I told him that I wanted us to take our time. I wanted to enjoy being engaged, and not hurried."

"Amen to that. I'm so happy for you both. Love looks good on you, girl. With all that's happened, you deserve to be happy for real. I knew Marcus was the real deal, but time had to show you what I've known all this time. And although Ben's my brother, I always felt like he was the rebound guy, and we know how many of those relationships workout. I also knew once you found out about him and Kherington, divorce was inevitable. So when you guys told us, I wasn't shock."

"True. You know me so well. But going through this process made me see who Marcus truly was in of spite my feelings. I saw how Marcus loved me through his actions, and not just obligation. Marcus's love was like it had always been, consistent. He stood by me girl when anyone else would have dropped me like a bad habit and ran. The kind of danger that I was in, honey, that had to be love."

"What about Ben? I mean, I know that you guys are divorcing."

"What about him? Don't get me wrong. He'll always hold a special place in my heart, but that ship has sailed, and he's free to do whatever he wants."

"I hear what you're saying and I hate to ask, but are you sure that he's out of your system?"

"Completely. He and I had words after signing the divorce papers."

"Girl what? That's so unlike him."

"Yeah, well. He basically was like I didn't take accountability for my actions in our marriage failing like he had."

"Wow." She said.

"And I hadn't heard from him since. The last time we spoke is when he gave me the update on Kherington and that we will no longer be needing security."

"That was a relief for us all, girl. But I hate things ended with you all having words."

"It is what it is. Other than that good news, I hadn't heard from him, and I'm good with that. I haven't seen him at work or anywhere else."

"And you don't think that's strange?" She asked.

"Not really. I figured whatever he's doing has him locked in."

"That's for sure. I think TJ may have spoken to him a couple of times briefly, but not how they use to."

"Respectfully, not my monkey, not my circus. His actions no longer involve me. That's the next woman's problem and I wish her the absolute best."

"Well, alright then. Speak your truth sis. I hear you." She said.

"Now, what we need to talk about is your up-and-coming nuptials. How far have you gotten?"

"Not far. There's so much to do, but at least we have a date set."

"That's a good start. Have you checked with the church to see if your date was available?"

"No. I meant to ask TJ to check, but forgot. I'm just glad to have been talking to you for this long. That little girl in there is so demanding. She acts like her father." She said, laughing.

"No worries, sis, I got you. I'll confirm that for you right now. Just let me grab my phone and I'll get to work."

Chapter 20

KHERINGTON

Ben and I have been exchanging text messages for a while. I know that he's been very busy with business, but when he's not traveling, he makes it a priority to keep in touch with me. I love that he's never too busy for his family. With it being just me, the baby, and occasionally nagging Phillip, I do get a little lonely. Hearing his voice made me miss him that much more every time we talk. Now that things are over between him and his ex-wife, he can focus on me, his future wife and what's good for our family. I just know that we are going to have a happy life. I already have my wedding dress picked out, but where would we get married? I should have changed my identity when I bought the social security card and birth certificate for the baby.

Ben wants to see me and the baby just as much as we want to see him. I can just see us now, cozied up on the sofa by the fire, watching family movies with our son. We will be the perfect little family. I will be glad when he comes home, too. Maybe he can do something about Phillip. He is driving me insane. Talk, talk, talk that's all he does, causing my headaches to become worser by the day. I wish he would go away permanently. I even tried to make peace with him by offering him something to eat, but he refuses to touch his plate. I tried to convince him that I had not poisoned it by tasting it first, but no. He'd rather stand up there complaining about what I was doing all day long. Just getting on my nerves for no reason. I told him to suit himself because Ben and I were going to be a real family and there was nothing he could do about it.

I guess he got the picture because I hadn't seen or heard a word from him all day. I don't know where he goes when he's not around, but my head sure does thank him whenever he leaves. He's a pain in more ways than one.

Every time he shows up, my head starts to hurt, but right

now I was feeling pretty good. I wasn't sure how long I

could keep taking this pain medication at such a high dose,

but I had to do whatever I could to take care of our son and

keep those headaches away. I felt so good that I even took

the baby outside today just to get some fresh air. We sat in

one of the rockers on the front porch. Being in the woods

was so peaceful. There was not another soul around for

miles. This was true country living. I was so lucky to have

found this home when I did. Well, I didn't exactly find it,

but I overheard someone talking about it when I sat with

the other doctors at lunch one night. This doctor was

bragging about how he had just left here with some woman

he had been seeing. He told us that it was very quiet and

serene, and he was absolutely right about that. It was no

one to see and nothing to do. Just me, the baby, and nature,

just like I liked it. The house reminded me of a wooden

cabin. The owner rented out their vacation home as an Airbnb. It was great for the perfect getaway. It sat back away from the street. If it weren't for the driveway, you wouldn't know that the house was there. I could tell that the owner had put in a lot of work in this place. It had all the up-to-date amenities.

When the baby had fallen asleep, I laid him down and rolled my garbage can down to the end of my long driveway. I was just in time, too. The garbage truck just pulled up to dump my trash.

"Good afternoon, ma'am. How are you doing today?" The garbage man asked.

"I'm doing well." I replied. "How are you?"

"I can't complain. It won't do me no good, anyway." He said, emptying my garbage bin.

"That's true."

"If you don't mind me asking, ma'am, you must be new around here?" He asked after placing my garbage can in front of me.

"I am." I confirmed.

"I figured. I've never seen you before, but you'll like the area. Everyone is so nice and friendly." He said before hopping on the back of the truck. "You have yourself a good day, ma'am, and don't you lose that beautiful smile."

"Thank you, and you do the same." I said, watching the truck leave.

That was awfully nice of him. I thought as I walked back to the house. Just as I placed the garbage can in the kitchen, Ben called.

"Hello." I answered.

"Hey what are you guys up to?"

"Your son is taking a nap, and I just finished hearing how beautiful my smile was." I said, blushing.

"Huh, your smile? Who told you that?" He asked.

"The garbage man." I said proudly.

"He saw your face? What if he recognizes you?"

"Yes, and no. I'm not worried. I always wear a baseball cap and shades. Are you jealous?" I asked, teasing him.

"Yes, and I don't appreciate some random man flirting with my woman."

"Stop it. He was just being friendly. Besides, you're the only man for me."

"I better be. When can I see you guys?"

"I'm not sure Ben." I replied.

"You're not sure about being with me? You'd rather be with Mr. Garbage Man. After everything we've been through, you're not sure? I'm not believing this." He said angrily.

"Listen, calm down. I'm sure, but I just don't want anything to happen. Don't be angry with me. You know how much I love you." I told him.

"I can't tell. Baby, you know I won't let anything happen to you and the baby. I need to be with my family right now. Why are you doing this to me? You know that you are all that I have. Are you going to deny me my family, too?"

"I'm nothing like them, and I would never deny you anything." I said angrily.

"Prove it. I want to see you all today." He demanded.

"Fine. I'm sending you the address. I can't wait to see you, baby. I really do love you. Don't you ever question my love for you." I said before hanging up to text him the address.

I can't wait to see Ben. It's been way too long. There was so much I had to do to prepare for his arrival, but first let me see what I was going to wear and cook. I wanted to do all the things he and I talked about, and what I constantly day dreamed about. I didn't know if I should greet him in lingerie or just something soft and pretty. But was I supposed to eat dinner naked? I'll circle back to that one. I should plan for a hearty meal. I thought as I was looking at what was available in the freezer. Whatever I was serving had to be thawed, and quickly. I only had an hour to get his meal prepared. Placing the steaks in hot water should help get things moving faster, but if I bake the meat, it can cook and thaw it at the same time. I ran hot water over the package so it would release the meat and seasoned it with salt and pepper. I didn't have all those other seasonings that I saw in the video. It took no time to place it in the oven. That left me with more than enough time to decide on what to wear, and finish preparing for his visit.

Chapter 21

BENJAMIN

Adrenaline rushed through my vines as I spoke to Kherington. I was willing to say just about anything to convince her to let me see them, and it finally paid off, too. Thank god! My phone had just beeped. "She sent the address." I told the agents that were in the room with me. My heart felt like it was about to jump right out of my chest. I felt like I had just hit the game winning shot. This moment is what took me away from everyone. I had to lock in and really focus to get to this point.

"Job well done, Benjamin!" One agent said.

"Thank you." I said.

"We are verifying that this is a match to her actual location."

"Good. I believe the compliment your undercover agent gave her helped me to seal the deal. He Jason Kidd that thing with his assist." I said.

"That was some damn good work, Harris. You almost had me convinced. You sure we can't recruit you to join the agency?" Agent Collins said.

"I'm positive. This was all about placing the baby back in the arms of his parents. I would do whatever it took to get him there." I told them.

"Now that we have ears on the garbage can, we can monitor what's going on from the inside."

"That's good. What's next?" I asked.

"Now that we have an address match, we are going to move into the next phase by having you meet her. Remember Benjamin, the goal is for her to come outside to you. We want you to lure her away from the house so that my team can go inside to rescue the baby, and then arrest her. Any questions so far?" He asked.

"No, I'm clear."

"You don't have to worry about anything Benjamin, we'll all be there, plus those that are already in position to go in at a moment's notice. Are you ready?" He said.

"Yes, let's go rescue a baby." I said.

Before leaving, we went over the plan one more time so that everyone would be on the same page. I understood the assignment the first time, and although I was nervous, I was ready to go. At this point, I had nothing to lose but everything to gain. Getting Cameron back was my only priority. He was the only thing I kept my focus on. Getting Kherington to come outside wouldn't be hard. She hung on every word I said. I sold her a dream so unbelievable that she'd have to be insane to even consider it. Talking to her, I learned that she switched her attention to me the night she came into Horizons asking about Phillip. She told me she knew that he was out of town. She said she used that as an excuse to get closer to me. She admitted that she and Phillip weren't in contact the way she said they had been, and that she invited herself to our Christmas party. Phillip had no clue that she'd be there. I asked her why she killed him. She confessed that he was in the way of her getting what she wanted. That he would stop me from seeing her, and she couldn't have that. That was the eeriest conversation I've ever had in my life. It was as if she had forgotten that he was deceased.

Chapter 22

TAMARA

My mother had been blowing my phone up all day.
So I had to take her next call before she drove to Alabama.
She had me worried because she'd never called me like this
before.

"Hey Ma," I answered quickly.

"Don't hey Ma me. I've been calling you all day,
girl."

"I know. I've been in back-to-back meetings all
day. What's going on?"

"What's going on? Chile, have you been watching
the news?"

"The news?" I know this woman hasn't been
blowing up my phone about the news. "No, why?" I asked
her.

"Chile, they on their talking about that guy that was in your wedding. What's his name, Tammy? Cause honey I don forgot. What's that baby's name, Lawd? They mentioned the company that y'all work for too. They almost made me burn my biscuits this morning watching them."

"Okay, what about Phillip and the company?" I already knew where this was heading.

"They were talking about the woman that killed him. I didn't know that the man was dead. I saw where they have some leads or something. Honey, what is this world coming to, and how come you didn't tell me about it? I had to get it from the news. I was telling them at work all about it."

"You wouldn't believe it if I told you."

"What do you mean?" She asked.

"Ma, so much has happened within the past few months that led up to all of this. It's just crazy."

"What happened Tammy?" She asked, concerned.

"Well, for starters, Ben and I have divorced." I confessed.

"What? Wait, I'm so confused. Why would y'all get a divorce, and how come I'm just learning about it?"

"Yes ma'am, I know that I should've told you, but I didn't want to worry you, mama. But the truth is, Ben and I both stepped outside of our marriage and I thought it best that we divorce. He and I agreed and did so as friends. I will be overseeing the foundation that we started in honor of his business partner and our friend, Phillip. The woman that killed him was his ex-girlfriend. Along with murder, she is wanted for kidnapping an infant."

"I help you to say so much has happened. Lawd have mercy on us, Jesus." She said.

"But wait, there's more."

"Uh-uh Tammy, I don't think I can handle anymore." She said.

"When Ben and I separated, Marcus allowed me to stay with him until I found another place."

"Un-huh," she said.

"And during that time, he and I rekindled our relationship and are now engaged."

She said nothing. "Hello." I said.

"Un-huh. I'm here." she said.

"Did you hear what I said?"

"Every word." She confirmed.

"And you don't have anything to say about it?" I asked, thrown off.

"You know how you might have reservations about something, but you keep it to yourself?"

"Yes, ma'am."

"Well, that's how I felt about you marrying Benjamin. Something just didn't sit well to me. I just couldn't point my finger on it. And don't get me wrong, I thought that he was a nice man from a wonderful family, but something just wasn't right. Marcus is someone that I have known and loved for years. I don't think you knew this, but he and I kept in touch even when y'all didn't. I still talked to his mother and aunt. Honey, we hang-out and everything."

"What? He never told me."

"Yeah, chile, we came to the conclusion that you were just acting out because you were a spoiled brat. But what we didn't account for was you marrying someone else. You weren't supposed to do that, but I am glad that you have finally come back to your senses. I've always thought that he was the perfect man for you."

"I can't believe this." I said.

"Un-huh, I know it. Now me and Gladys and the girls can help plan a wedding for real."

"Slow your role, Cookie. He and I aren't in any hurry. As I told Erica, I want to enjoy my engagement this time. I'm not in any rush to get married."

"There you go again, thinking about yourself. What about us? The ones that have been waiting on beautiful grandbabies."

"They'll come in due time. I promise."

"I just hope that we aren't feeble or dead and gone before they do. We want to be able to play and do things with them."

"I can't win with you, lady. I was just calling you back to see what was going on and how you were doing."

"Honey, I'm feeling great now that I know that you're okay, and I officially got my son back. Wait until I tell Gladys and Cherry about this."

"Handle your business ma'am, I'm about to leave the office and head home. I love you."

"I love you too, and tell Marc that I love him the most." She said, laughing.

"Oh, really?"

"Girl, you almost got disowned by mistreating my baby. I love me some him, me and his other mama."

"A mess. I'll talk to you later, ma."

"Bye Tammy." She said before hanging up.

How are you going to disown your child for someone else's? I can't with her. And wouldn't you know it? I was being FaceTimed by my replacement.

"Hello trader." I answered.

"Well, hello to you too, Mrs. Worthington. How are you doing today?" He said, laughing.

"I was doing pretty good until I learned from my mother that she was thinking about disowning me for you." I said, rolling my eyes. "Oh yeah, she told me to tell you that she loves you the most."

"Don't be jealous because I'm the son-in-law she's always wanted. That's my girl and she don't play about me, so you better be good to me, or I'm going to have to tell on you."

"Whatever. I'm not thinking about you or Cookie. How was your day?" I asked, ignoring his little comment.

"Pretty cool. I'm on call tonight, so do you want to come hangout with me?"

"At the hospital?" I asked.

"Yep, like we used to do back in the day."

"No, sir." I said, laughing.

"Come on. I moved up from a sofa to a bunk bed. I have more space now." He said as if that would make the offer sweeter.

"How about this? I'll bring you dinner and we'll eat together. How does that sound?"

"Boring. What happened to my whenever, wherever, girl?"

"She became the CEO, face, and brand of a foundation, knowing she can't afford to be caught having sex in the doctor's mess with her fiancé."

"Fine. But you must admit that we used to have some good times."

"Yes, we did, but what you're forgetting is how many times that we were almost caught."

He laughs, "Yeah, those were some exciting times. But that's what happens when you have young and single interns on the prowl. Believe it or not, it's still happening. I just share my bunk with another doctor that's married. He lives close by, and rarely sleeps here."

"There's nothing like the comfort of you own bed." I said.

"Since you don't want to stay the night with me, you'll have to make it up to me when I get home in the morning."

"If I'm awake." I teased him.

"Trust me, I got you on that too." He said, winking at me.

Blushing, I said, "Anyway, what do you want for dinner?" He got over smiling like crazy. If his waking me was anything like this morning, I can't wait to go to turn in for the night.

"Surprise me. Just make sure it isn't anything heavy. I try to stay away from heavy foods at night just in case I do get some sleep."

"What about a nice salad and salmon on the side?"

"I'd rather have you on the side, but that will work, too." He flirted.

"Okay, babe, you're doing too much." I said, laughing. "I'll see you soon with dinner."

That chocolate man of mine knew how to make me smile, and I'll have the rest of my life to thank him for it.

Chapter 23

KHERINGTON

Ben just called to say that he was ten minutes away and I'm so excited. Just as I planned, everything was finally coming together. I wanted to welcome my man to his new home by cooking him a steak dinner. The funny thing is I've never cooked anything like this before, so I hope everything is to his liking. I would have ordered us something, but I didn't want to risk being seen by anyone. So this has to work. I can make simple things, but this was a welcomed challenge, I guess. I should have made something easier, like eggs and toast, but who would want to come home to that? I watched enough cooking videos to think that I did it right, but he'll have to be the judge of it. I think I may have over cooked my rice because it's sticky and hard to get out of the pot. My broccoli didn't look too bad. I cooked it in the microwave on high for five minutes,

I put a little salt and pepper on it. He's going to be so happy when he sees the delicious meal I prepared for us. Shoot, I forgot to make the gravy for the rice. Oh well, butter will have to do the trick.

I pulled the steak out of the oven and turned the stove off just in time. I heard a car pull into the driveway. I can't believe that he was here. I plated our food and sat them on the table, but when Ben hadn't rung the doorbell, I became concerned. So, I peeped out of the window to make sure that it was his car, and thankfully it was. I instantly became nervous at the mere thought of my man finally being here with me.

Curiosity had gotten the best of me. I started to wonder what was taking him so long to come to the door, but before I could get the thought out good, he called me on the phone.

"Hello." I answered.

"Hey babe, can you come outside so that I know that I'm at the right house?"

"Here I come." I said, laughing.

Before going outside to meet Ben, I checked on the baby, who was still fast asleep, and checked myself out in the mirror. Somehow I had turned back the hands of time. I was the same size as I was in college. With the weight loss, my clothes fit baggy, but that was okay. With Ben being here, I'll eat better meals for sure, and not just snack like I'd been doing. I'll make sure that we have healthy, plentiful meals every day. If there's a video for it, I can cook it, or at least try, I thought as I went outside.

"Ben, I can't believe that you are here!" I yelled from the front porch. "What are you doing?" I asked him, as it appeared that he was looking in his trunk for something. Why did he park mid-way up the driveway I wondered?

"Hey baby! It's good to see you, too. I bought you and the baby something and I'm just having a hard time getting it out of the car. Can you come and help me? I believe it got caught on something." He said.

"Sure, I can't wait to see what you bought for us." I said, walking towards his car. "Why did you park so far back, though?" I asked, walking down the driveway.

"I wasn't sure if I was at the right house or not. Girl, you just can't go walking up on random porches. That's a guaranteed way of getting shot. Especially out here. How did you find this place, anyway?" He said, peeking around the trunk as I walked down the driveway.

"Boy, you are so crazy." I said, laughing.

"Stop right there. Before you come any closer, close your eyes." He said.

"What? How am I going to help you with my eyes closed?"

"I want you to be surprised, but before I do, I'm going to give you the biggest, tightest hug because I've missed you that much. Are you ready?" He asked sweetly.

"Yes." I said, squirming like a little schoolgirl.

"Okay now, no peeking." He said.

When that man wrapped his big arms around me, I melted like chocolate. His hug was not like it was before. He was so strong, so reassuring, so confidant. I'd never been held like this before, and I just wanted him to have his way with me, right here, right now. He held me like he never wanted to let me go. But before I could move in for my kiss, someone had forcefully pulled me away from my love and onto the ground. Laying on my stomach, I kicked and squirmed to break free, but it was too late. I opened my eyes and realized it wasn't Ben at all who held me so close and tight. It was the garbage man from earlier wearing a bullet proof vest dressed in all black. He was standing next to Ben watching as I was arrested. If I hadn't had my hands handcuffed behind my back, I would have made Ben pay for crossing me.

One officer read me my rights as they walked me to the police car, and another patted me down for concealed weapons before being placing me in the backseat. In silence, I sat there and watched out of the window in disbelief when I saw Ben hand our baby boy over to the surrogate. I couldn't believe it. I noticed the man standing next to her. He looked just liked our baby. Suddenly it hit me like a thousand lightning bolts. Ben was not the father at all. He had me to kidnap someone else's child and now I was going to prison for it.

"How could you do this to me? I loved you!" I shouted at him. I risked it all for him. We were supposed to be a family, and he betrayed me like this. "He was supposed to love me the same way I loved him, and without judgement," I cried out, but no one cared to listen or hear me.

All of my hopes and dreams came crashing down to my feet at the revelation of his betrayal. I felt waves of rage overtaking me. I could no longer control my thoughts or emotions. I was drowning in a sea of treachery. He'd betrayed me, ran through my mind a million times. He had lied to me did the same thing a million times more.

"I told you so," Phillip said, sitting next to me, gloating.

I screamed and screamed and screamed until I passed out.

Chapter 24

Breaking News

"Hello, I'm Karen Starr at the news desk with breaking news. The suspect, Dr. Kherington Draker, was captured today and taken into police custody without incident where she is currently being hospitalized for a mental evaluation and psychiatric treatment. Upon her release, she will be transferred and charged in Jefferson County with murder in the first degree, attempted murder, kidnapping, credit card fraud, and other pending charges. We have Lacey James on location with more developing news. What more can you tell us, Lacey?"

"Yes, the four-month-old infant, Cameron Lassiter, who was kidnapped from Living Well Labs seven weeks ago, was found safe and unharmed in an isolated area in the city of Sylacauga. He, along with the alleged kidnapper, were both rushed to the Coosa Valley Medical Center for evaluations. The doctors later released the baby to his

parents. From another source close to the investigation

stated the alleged kidnapper had cared for the child as if he

were her own.”

"We are sorry to interrupt you, Lacey. There is a

news conference in progress going live. Lacey, please

standby. We are now joining the live press conference in

progress with the Birmingham Police Department.” The

newscaster said.

"This is a proud day for law enforcement

everywhere. We are thankful to all the agencies that came

together and rallied around this family. It has been a

hellacious few weeks for them. This arrest took the help of

our beloved community, who provided detailed information

that led to the suspect’s capture. We are also glad to be able

to bring justice to the Gray family. The victim, Phillip

Gray, was a pilar of this community and did not deserve to

die the way that he had. The suspect had evaded us at every

turn, but she made a fatal mistake that allowed us not only to find her, but to monitor her every movement. We here at the Birmingham Police Department wanted to return the infant home to his family, and we have done so safely. At this time, our investigation is still ongoing, and I will be taking a few questions pertaining to the case." The Chief of Police K. Nasser said.

"ABC News. Do you know the condition of the suspect at this time?"

"No. Last reported the suspect was undergoing a psych evaluation and possible treatment."

"CBS News. Do you think the suspect will stand trial if they are undergoing a psych evaluation?"

"At this time, we do not have any reason to suggest that she wouldn't. We are law enforcement, not attorneys or judges."

"FOX News. Were there any specific tips reported by the community that led to the suspect's arrest? Did you all go buy a single tip, or were there multiples?"

"There were many tips provided by the community. Some even helpful, but by multiple agencies working together is what led to the suspect's capture and arrest."

"NBC News. Are there any other suspects that you are looking at, or do you all believe the suspect acted alone?"

"The investigation is still ongoing and at this time, the suspect in custody is the main subject of our investigation. That's all of the questions for today. Thank y'all." The chief said before walking away from the podium.

"Can you tell us where the suspect and child were found?" A reporter yelled out.

"Do you know what psychological issues the suspect is having?" Another yelled.

"What did the parents say when they first saw their child?" Yelled out from the back of the room.

"That was the chief of police taking a few questions from news reporters. We have Lacey back with more, Lacey." She said.

"Thanks Karen. I contacted little Cameron's parents earlier today. His mother, Stacey Johnson, expressed her gratitude, saying. "I am so thankful to have my son back in my arms, and to everyone who helped to return him home safely." When asked about the woman that took her child, she said she is looking forward to justice being served. She says, "No parent should ever have to experience the trauma and worry that they had." Reporting live from Sylacauga, I'm Lacey James with your local news."

"Thank you, Lacey. What an amazing story. I'm glad to hear that the little guy is back home safe with his parents. We all could use more good news like this. The weather and other news after the break." Karen said.

Chapter 25

STACEY

When Ben placed Cameron in my arms, all I could

do was hold him and cry. We were escorted to the location

of where Cameron was being kept. It was all I could do not

to get out of that car before time. Andrew held my hand as

to say don't move, but when I saw Ben carrying my baby to

the end of that driveway, I couldn't stay. Before I knew it,

Andrew was holding both of us, as we cried tears of joy.

We left the scene, and the paramedics transported

us to the hospital with Cameron. While we were there, the

police brought in the person who kidnapped him. I was told

that she had suffered some sort of psychotic episode and

had to be rushed to the hospital. We waited to find out

when she would be released for arraignment, but at that

time, no one had any information. It was still too early to

tell due to her being evaluated. I was concerned that she

would be able to bail out of jail, but after speaking with some of the officers, they reassured me she wouldn't be able to post bail. They told me because of the charges pending against her, the judge would insist on her remaining in jail on what they called a no bond order. I was so relieved to hear that.

A month or so had passed when we received a phone call providing us with the date and time of Kherington's arraignment. It was a packed courtroom, too. Andrew and I sat two rows behind the plaintiff's table, and Ben and Pastor Harris were sitting on the end on the next row behind us. The woman that walked through that door looked like she had been through hell and back. She was shackled in chains wearing an orange jumpsuit. She looked nothing like the woman that flashed across every tv screen in America. This woman was now a fraction of her former self. She looked like she had been mentally tortured.

When she looked up and saw us sitting across the room, she began to yell at us.

"You stole my baby!" She shouted.

"Order in the court!" The judge said, slamming his gavel against the wooden pad. "Mr. Rutherford, please control your client, or I will have to clear the courtroom."

"Where is my baby? Give me back my baby!" She yelled, trying to break free from the officers who were holding her. And somehow she broke free from them and charged at Ben. **"Benjamin Harris, I'm going to kill you!"** She was only inches away from him when they wrestled her down to the ground. This sent the court room into chaos. **"He did it! He did it! He made me do it! He's the one that needs to be in jail."** Kherington yelled at the top of her lungs.

Shock and fear paralyzed Ben.

"Please don't hurt my daughter!" An older

woman stood and cried out in fright as an older man

standing with her looked on.

"Your honor in light of this, we would like to

request a competency hearing." Her attorney said, as we

witnessed Kherington being restrained and carried out of

the courtroom. You could hear her screaming as she went

down the hall.

"The motion is granted. Court is adjourned." The

judge said.

After the incident, I spoke to Ben and Pastor Harris.

I thanked Ben for helping to get Cameron back, and I

apologized for hitting him. I think what Kherington had

said and done did something to him. I could tell that he was

not himself.

"Are you okay?" I asked him.

"Umm, yeah. I'm good. Thanks for asking."

"That was something, wasn't it?" I asked him.

"It definitely was, but um, we're gonna go ahead and leave. You two take care." He said.

"You too, man." Andrew said.

"Excuse me." The older couple from the courtroom said, catching Ben before he could leave. "I'm not sure if you remember us, but we are Kherington's parents."

"Mr. and Mrs. Draker. It's been years." He said, smiling.

"We wanted to speak to you all. We know that there's nothing we can do to fix the reprehensible actions of our daughter, but on behalf of our family, we would like to offer you all our sincerest apology. There is no excuse we could possibly give that would make sense at a time like this. We pray that the damage caused will not in any way, shape, or form, bring harm to your child." Mr. Draker said to me.

"We thank you and appreciate your prayers," Andrew said.

"I hope your daughter gets the help that she desperately needs." I genuinely said.

"You and I both. We don't want to hold you all up. We just couldn't leave without saying anything," Mrs. Draker said.

"Your family will be in our prayers as well. I got a chance to know your daughter." Pastor Harris said. "And for the life of me, I don't know what happened. Just know you all are in our prayers."

"Thank you." They said. "Benjamin, it was good to see you again. I just wished it was under better circumstances." Mrs. Draker said.

"I as well, but it was good seeing you both," Ben said, hugging her and shaking Mr. Draker's hand before we all dispersed.

***

Two weeks later, it was determined that Kherington was too incompetent to stand trial. I wanted her to pay for all the trauma she caused my family, but knowing she couldn't hurt us, or anyone else for that matter, gave me some solace.

In celebration of having Cameron home, we had a cookout at Big Mama's house. The men were in the backyard grilling, and most of the women were in the kitchen preparing the sides. I was in the den rocking my baby to sleep.

"Their you two are." My biological father Richard said.

"Hey. It's nap time for this one. I've been meaning to talk to you, too."

"And I you. Pastor Harris and I finally found time to meet. We had some scheduling conflicts before, but had lunch the other day, and he told me that we were almost relatives."

"Yeah, it was during one of my not so proud moments that I was briefly engaged to their son, Christopher."

"But what confuses me is how you ended up being with Benjamin, and how they didn't know about it? What, he never brought you around their family or something?"

"I can explain that." I said, laughing. "Ben and I had known each other for years prior to my meeting his brother. But the type of relationship Ben and I had, we didn't talk about our personal lives. We just randomly spent time together. So when I met Chris or Christopher, as you may know him, we were working on something real. I didn't know that they were brothers initially until he started telling me about his family. Chris mentioned having a successful younger brother and wanted to introduce me to him, but time never permitted him to do so until that faithful night at the club. I know I should have come clean with the both of them, but didn't. Since Ben was never around much, and Chris lived out of town, no one ran into each other."

"But two brothers, Stacey?" He asked.

"I know. I told Chris the truth about Ben and I the night he surprised him. And although Ben and I weren't in a relationship, he had done something that I thought was foul, so I repaid him by exposing the fact that I was engaged to his brother. Chris and I had not been engaged long before this happened. He had flown me out of town the weekend before and proposed marriage. We were in a solid relationship for a year before all of this ever happened, and what was crazier is how Ben ended up marrying someone I worked with. I figured that they may have known each other because of their friendship with TJ and Erica, but never them hooking up and marrying. Now that was wild." I said, reminiscing.

"I see. So you blew up everyone's life because of jealousy. And what's this I hear about you and Jasmine coming down to their church and causing a scene?"

"No sir. I was provoked that day. It was your other daughter that wanted to go their church to spy on TJ. I just went for the service and while I was there, Chris thought he would flex and show off in front of his woman. To tell you the truth, it was him that caused the scene and tried to be funny, but it blew up in his face. He thought he was doing something major."

"Lawd have mercy on my children." He said. "I understand what you are saying, but Stacey, that was still uncalled for. Pastor Harris told me it was scandalous. Christopher had to come before the congregation and apologize for making a scene."

"Oh yeah. So, what else did he say?" I asked, not caring about his little apology. I was the one he had offended. Where was my apology?

"That was enough. Why? Do you want to add more to the story?"

"No sir. I just wanted you to know that I was not the only bad apple of the bunch. I had help."

"Well, what did you want to talk to me about?"

"Andrew and I wanted to discuss having Cameron christened at the church."

"Oh yeah, we can definitely do that. When were you all thinking about doing it?"

"Next Sunday."

"Next Sunday it is. Anything else?" He asked.

"Yes. Um, Tracey and I have been talking about this and it's kind of uncomfortable to even ask you. Like to the point of being embarrassing."

"What is it?" He asked with worry on his face.

"Okay, here it goes." I said, taking a breath. "I wished Tracey was here to help me ask this question. Here it goes. What do we call you now? I mean, we've known you as Uncle Richard all of our lives, and to know you now as our biological father, we've just been wrestling with how to address you."

"Just call me Uncle-daddy." He said with a straight face. I guess by my facial expression caused him to burst out in laughter.

"That's not funny." I said, starting to laugh myself.

"I'm just playing, I'm just playing." He said, still laughing so hard and loud it almost woke my baby up. "Seriously, call me whatever you all feel. Who I am nor my love for the both of you will ever change. I've always called you my girls."

"Yes, you have. Thanks dad." I said, leaning over to kiss him on the cheek. "I'll call you Poppa Rich."

"That sounds good to me." He said.

"Hey y'all, everything is ready to eat," Aunt Carmen came in and said. "Hand me Mr. Handsome and I'll go lay him down in his baby bed."

"Thanks auntie." I said, as she took the baby from me. Despite our friction, she loved herself some Cameron, and would tell anyone who would listen that he was named after her.

"You're welcome sweetie. Y'all better get in there and fix your plates. I put mine to the side before coming in here. Y'all know we have a house full of hefty eaters.

"And do." Poppa Rich and I said in unison.

"Well, did anybody bother to bless the food?" He asked her.

"Un-huh," she said. "Right before they put the fork into their mouths."

"We better get in there." I said. "I don't hear anybody talking and you know what that means."

"Yeah, they're in there eating good." He said as we walked to the kitchen. "You know Andrew asked me for your hand in marriage?"

"He told me he would. He just didn't tell me what you said. He told me that was between you and him."

"I basically told him to be a better father to his son than I was to my daughters." I was shocked. "I also told him to shower you with the love that you rightfully deserved. Baby girl, I've made some mistakes in my lifetime, but one thing I can say is when things are meant to be, life has a way of bringing those things back around . So if you truly love this man, love him with intentionality. Love and support this man on purpose. And no matter what, sweetheart, be honest with him. I know how he feels about you because he shared that with me. All I ask is that you return the same love that is being given to you."

"I will. It took me some time to realize just what he truly meant to me. With him, there's no hiding. He unconditionally loves me. I couldn't have been blessed to have found a better man than Andrew."

"I'm pleased to hear it." He said.

"Hey babe, where's little man?" Andrew asked after kissing me on the cheek.

"Aunt Carmen laid him down for his nap."

"Cool. I fixed you a burger." He said, handing me the plate.

"See what I mean. Now my wife ain't did that and I've been married to her for thirty-plus years." He whispered in my ear.

I laughed. "What's going on?" Andrew asked.

"Poppa Rich and I were just saying how good of a man that you are."

"That's because I finally have the one that I wanted to be good to."

"And on that note, I'm going to put some potato salad on my plate before it's all gone." Poppa Rich said before walking off smiling.

We laughed. "Do you have everything you need before we go sit down?" I asked him.

"Yes, ma'am."

Andrew and I sat at the table next to Jas and Devontae and we talked about going on vacation and if we were going to take our kids along. We both had little babies to consider. Jas gave birth to identical twin boys, Chase and Chance. They were the cutest three-month-old babies I'd ever seen next to my baby. She was so shocked when they went to see what they were having. When the doctor said I hear two heartbeats, she screamed. I don't know why she was shocked, twins do run our family.

"There y'all go again making plans without me and Tracey." Keisha complained.

I wasn't in the mood. So I looked over at Jasmine for her to address it. "Keisha, what are you talking about? We do include you, but what do you do every time we say that we are planning to go on a trip?"

"It ain't my fault the timing is bad, plus I don't always have a babysitter. Y'all don't have that problem. All

I have is mama and daddy and they get tired of keeping my kids." She said.

"And as for Tracey, we don't forget about her either. She's always busy and you know that," Jasmine said.

"All I know is that y'all be leaving us out of stuff, just like y'all did the other day."

"The other day?" I blurted out. "Girl, she rode with me to pick up my prescription and we stopped by Ulta."

"And Starbucks. Y'all went to Starbucks without me." She said.

"You can't be for real? Jasmine, get your sister." I told her.

"Nah, you get your sister because that's just crazy."

"But y'all know how much I like Starbucks and y'all went without me."

"I can't believe she is mad at us for not taking her to Starbucks." I said.

"I can. We are talking about Keisha. You know she has to be included in everything." Jasmine said.

"And do. Y'all ain't gon keep talking about me like I'm not present." She said with an attitude.

"We all know that you are here. We can't help but to know that you're here. You're the only one here complaining about nothing. Now, if you want to go there so bad, come and pick me up tomorrow, and take me because I like their caramel frappuccino." Big Mama told her who had overheard the entire conversation.

"I'll have to check my schedule." Keisha told her. Knowing full well she had nothing to do.

We all burst out laughing because with Big Mama, Starbucks would be the last place you'd be going. She had to go to the bank first, then she had to go and pay a bill or two, hit three different grocery stores, because everyone of them had something on sale that she needed. And let's not forget Elyton's meat market. They were the only ones that cut her pork chops the way she liked them, and after all of those places, maybe then you'd go to Starbucks. I loved my family dearly, but they were a trip.

Later that night, Andrew made good on a promise. He proposed in front of our families. Tracey wasn't in town, but she was on FaceTime. I gladly excepted his proposal, and would have married him right away, had Poppa Rich not suggested we take marriage counseling. I started to say, "We don't need that," but thinking back on my past relationships, yes, we did.

In the past, I could only pretend to be a wife. There was no need to pretend anymore. I had a man in my life that saw a wife in me. He truly loved me. I didn't have to prove to him that I was worthy. He saw it. I didn't have to have sex with him to show me attention. He gave it to me. So, how could I not do what was necessary to make our marriage last? We already knew what it took to keep things spicy in the bedroom. We had Cameron as proof of that.

What I lacked was the experience of loving on purpose, and not for what you could do for me. Other than my brief engagement with Chris, I had never experienced love in this way. I wanted a marriage like I saw growing up. I saw the love between my parents and grandparents. I saw how my aunts and uncles loved and supported one another. I missed out on how they achieved it. Even in their ups and downs, they found a way to make things work. This is what I wanted to learn. This is what I needed to know.

Not that I thought Andrew would ever give up on me, but fear drove me to ask the what ifs. What if he one day decides that marriage is no longer working for him? What do I do? What if I decided to change my mind? What would he do? I wanted this to be be my first and last marriage. I wanted Cameron to grow-up in a loving two-parent home surrounded by love just like I did. I wanted to teach him that through the worst of times, his

parents held each other down.

Chapter 26

BENJAMIN

Although some months had passed, I could still hear

Kherington's spine tingling screams. I've never heard

anyone scream like that in my life. I wanted to call Stacey

and check in on them, but I thought it best to leave things

as they were. Cameron was back at home with his parents

and that's all that mattered to me. When I handed him over

to her, it was all I could do to keep my emotions in check. I

was just glad to see that my hard work had paid off. He, on

the other hand wasn't too happy about being awakened

from his nap, but he had some people that needed to see

that he was okay, and I was one of them.

I had so much bottled up emotionally and nowhere

to unload it. This emotional baggage of mine drained me,

and I desperately needed someone to talk to. The death of

Phillip, my divorce from Tamara, and the kidnapping of

Cameron all weighed me down. My dad suggested that

seek out counseling because to him, I didn't seem like

myself, and he was right. I needed to decompress. So I

received a recommendation from a friend. They suggested

that I make an appointment with Dr. Smith. Before making

my appointment, I did my research. I saw that he had

excellent ratings from his patients. Many people highly

recommended him. One comment said that he was a good

therapist that was very relatable to his patients. After

reading many reviews, I chose to contact Dr. Smith's

office. I believed he could help me, and I made my appoint

to see him that day. It didn't take long at all. His office

asked me a few questions over the phone, and after that, his

office emailed me forms to fill out regarding my medical

history. All that was left to do was show up and now I'm

here.

"Mr. Harris, what brings you in today?" He asked.

"Where do I begin, Dr. Smith? So much has happened within the past six months. I've basically lost my way and the people that were significant to me. Like five years ago, I had a plan. I knew what I wanted and who would be around when I got there, but right now that vision isn't so clear anymore."

"Why do you think that is?"

"Well, for starters, my business partner died."

"My condolences."

"Thank you. He was not just a business partner, but a good friend as well. Would you believe he and I got into a physical altercation hours before his death?"

"Why was that?" He asked, concerned.

"I was a hothead, and we fought, well I fought him because I felt like he had disrespected me."

"What made you think that he had?"

"He had been with my wife. I'm sorry, my ex-wife sexually."

"Did you all divorce because of the affair?"

"No, we divorced because she said she could never trust me again."

"And why did she say that if she was the one who had the affair?"

"Because I had cheated on her twice. Once before we got married and the second time during."

"I see. Do you find it difficult to be committed to one person while you're in a relationship?"

"To be honest, my ex-wife was my first real committed relationship. Before her, I causally dated. I wasn't looking for anything serious until I met her." I told him. "Now, she's engaged to her ex."

"How do you feel about that?"

"It hurts like hell because even though she had slept with my friend, I'd forgiven her because of everything we'd been through. I did everything I could to fix things."

"How did you try to fix it?"

"By manipulation. I found out my ex-wife and the woman I had been seeing before her worked together. So I had my then business partner ask her to join our company, and when I made the mistake of sleeping with that woman, again, I asked my ex-wife to marry me, because the woman ended up being pregnant."

"Why didn't you just come clean about everything?"

"Because I was afraid that she would leave me."

"So by asking her to marry you, you were hoping to prevent the inevitable?"

"I honestly did. I thought that if she had found out that she wouldn't leave me because we were already married. We both had this thing about staying married."

"Did she ever find out?"

"Yes, that's what led up to her sleeping with my friend. He was her shoulder to cry on."

"Having a shoulder to cry on doesn't necessarily lead to the bedroom. There had to be something more going on long before that led them there. Not saying that it was because I don't know them. Most things start out innocently enough, and then something happens to change the course."

"I can see that. That's exactly what I believed happened between Kherington and I."

"Which one is she the before or during your marriage?"

"She was the one who was my sounding board when my ex-wife refused to listen to me. I turned to her for support, because she was going through something similar, or so I thought. I later learned that it was all a wicked game that she played to get next to me."

"It sounds like you've been through a great deal."

"I have, and I blame myself for it. I feel like it is my karma. One manipulation led to a death, divorce, and kidnapping."

"That's a heavy burden to place on yourself. Many participated, not just you. If you don't mind me asking, how did your friend die?"

"Kherington poisoned him and tried to do the same to my ex-wife."

"Why would she poison your friend?"

"I'm sorry. I forgot to mention that they were in an on again off again type of relationship. When he died, he'd put a final end to them and there was no coming back."

"So, this Kherington woman was in a relationship with your friend, and this same friend also slept with your ex-wife, and then the two of you slept together? Did I get that right?"

"Yes, sir."

"An entanglement indeed. And where is this young woman today?"

"Spending the rest of her life in a psych ward. I'm not sure if you follow the news, but she was the one the police was looking for as a murder suspect. Her name is Dr. Kherington Draker."

"I remember something faintly about that case. She kidnapped a baby also, didn't she?"

"Yes, she did. It was from the woman whom I was seeking a paternity test."

"My goodness. So she's currently in the psych ward?"

"Yes, her defense was able to prove that she was mentally incompetent to stand trial. When the FBI searched the home, they found enough supplies to last for months. With everything she had accumulated, they found more arsenic and this time chloroform. During her brief interrogation, she was asked about the chloroform's purpose. She didn't utter a single word. I was told all she did was sit there and smiled at the agents. It was as if they were speaking another language other than English to her. I was also informed about the poorly cooked dinner she had prepared for me." I told him.

"Wow. That's a tough pill to swallow. Nevertheless, she will be there for the rest of her life."

"I'm just glad that this nightmare is finally over." I said

"That makes two of us. I'm glad that you came in today, Benjamin. We have a lot to unpack, but no worries, we'll get there. I would like for you to make your next appointment with my receptionist before leaving today. If you need anything, please do not hesitate to contact my office. I will see you next time."

"Thank you, Dr. Smith. I'm feeling better already."

"That's what I love to hear." He said, walking me to the door.

This was the first time in a long time that I felt like

things were getting back on track.

Chapter 27

TJ

I was about three-sheets in the wind before realizing what had Ben acting like a grumpy old man. It was my wedding day and he couldn't get into the celebration because of Tamara and Marcus. He acted a damn donkey when he thought I had added the man as a groomsman, and I wouldn't have. Marcus and I had always been cool, but I knew how Ben felt. Their divorce was finalized only a few months ago. It appeared that she had moved on with her life, and he was sulking in his. I knew how much he really loved her, but sometimes you have to be man enough to take an L. Especially if you were the blame.

"Are you going to sit here and be in your feelings all night?" I asked Ben.

"I might. I have nothing else better to do."

"What about that young lady you were talking to earlier?"

"Erica's co-worker? She's cool. I'm not trying to get into anything though." He said.

"Ben, you need to snap out of it, bro. We're at my reception. You know we supposed to be turning up."

"You go ahead, bro. I'm straight right here."

"You're straight right where? Sitting in a corner, alone, looking like somebody has put you on punishment."

"I'm just chilling."

"Chilling you are not. You have fury written all over your face," Ce said, sitting next to us.

"I'm telling y'all. I'm chilling."

"If you say so, bro. I'm just saying it's too many available women in the room to be sitting over here all alone." I told him.

"Yeah Ben, I agree with TJ. I saw how dryly you spoke to them, man. You're wearing your feelings on your sleeve. Clearly she's moved on and you need to do the same."

"Y'all don't get it. It's not that easy for me. I'm really having a hard time trying to figure out why it was so easy for her? I messed up, yeah, but to be engaged to someone else within a matter of months is crazy to me. I'm thinking, like had she been playing me this entire time? I'm starting to question everything."

"Man, you can't let what she does affect you."

"I wasn't, at first, but now, it's right here in my face. How could I not think about it?"

"It's going to take some time, bro. I know how you feel. I was in love with Stacey and finding out what happened between the two of you hurt me deeply, but I didn't allow that to stop me from finding Felecia. And you can't allow her engagement to stop you."

"You're right, Ce. Look fellas, I'm going to call it a night. TJ hit me up when y'all return from your honeymoon. Ce, I'll get with you later."

"Alright man, be easy." I told him.

"I will." Ben said before leaving.

"Wow bro, he has it bad."

"Yeah man. All we can do is give him time to work through it." Ce said as we watched Ben leave.

Chapter 28

TAMARA

Butterflies fluttered in my belly as we began welcoming patients in the building. I was nervous, but I felt wonderful. It was like I worked my whole life to be where I was, and despite everything that was lost to get here, I've gained so much more. I only wished Phillip was here to see what I was able to accomplish with his dream. He'd be so proud. He often talked about opening up a facility to help people who had mental health issues. Our facility offered the best outpatient holistic to medical methods imaginable.

"Good morning." I said to one. "Welcome." I said to another as I made my way back to my office.

I was getting ready to reply to an email when my secretary called.

"Ms. Reed, you have a visitor." She said.

"Okay, send them in." I told her. I knew it wasn't
Marcus because he was in surgery at the moment. "Come
in." I said to the knock at the door.

"Hello, Ms. Reed." He said as handsome as ever.

"Wow, what do I owe the pleasure, Mr. Harris?" I
asked. The last time I saw him, it was a blasé hello, and a
very dry, good to see you type of greeting. I'm shocked
he's visiting me today. I figured after our divorce, he'd
want nothing to do with me.

"Now, you know good and well that I was not going
to come by and congratulate you on your grand opening. I
apologize that I couldn't make it to your launch event. I
was out of town that day. I stopped by briefly to let you
know how proud of you that I was, and I know Phillip
would feel the same way."

"Ben, thank you so much. I appreciate that. I just
want to do an excellent job for the people and see his dream

fulfilled. I feel like I owe him this. He had done so much to help me. I can only hope that I have made him proud."

"And you will. I have no doubt about that. The building looks really good. You all did a great job rehabbing this place." He said, looking around my office and taking a sit.

"Thank you. That's what I was so nervous about the most. The permits, and passing the building inspections. When Mother Gray saw it, she cried. She and your parents came to the ribbon cutting ceremony. They're so sweet, too. Pop told me no matter what, that I was still his daughter."

"So you move in on my parents while I'm out of town."

"Absolutely not. They just love me. Oh, before I forget. Thank you for the flowers you sent, too. They were beautiful." I told him.

"That was nothing. Thank you for agreeing to be on the board of trustees for H & G."

"I'm honored to do it. I made H & G Investment my home, and although I'm not there with you all, the foundation is an affiliate of the company. So we're still connected, and I wouldn't have it any other way." I told him.

"Okay, can we stop with the professional pleasantries and get to the real?"

"Yes, please." I said, lowering my head and blowing out air. I could only take this for so long. We didn't have a reason to impress one another, neither were we strangers.

"I meant what I said. I'm so proud of you. You have done an amazing job with the foundation, plus with what you have going on, you could possibly franchise."

"Whoa, let me get this off the ground first. I almost pulled my hair with this one."

"Just food for thought. You have something worthwhile going on here."

"Thanks Ben. I'll take what you said under strong consideration. How are things going at the firm?"

"Everything is going smooth. I don't have to travel as much, but when I do, I'm gone for a minute. I'm working on something in L.A. and it's a possibility that I will open up another office and relocate there. This would give me the ability to handle things on the west coast."

"Oh wow. Look at you making moves. I see you, Mr. Harris."

"Thanks, but other than that, everything is cool."

"That's good. I was worried."

"Why? You hand picked and trained your replacement, and I must say, Maxwell is phenomenal. With the exception of Ms. Hopkins, we're an all boy's club."

"Don't y'all go running my girl off."

"Too late. She's retiring at the end of the month. She said I had run off her baby, and she was leaving too."

"What!?" I asked.

"I'm just playing. She didn't say that, but she really is retiring. I wonder if the new person will know how to bake muffins? One lady I saw that came through there looked mean. I wouldn't want her to make me anything, not even coffee."

"You're stupid. I just want you to know that." I said, laughing at him.

"She did. But listen, I'm going to roll out and let you get back to work. I just wanted to stop by for a minute. I got a conference call to hop on in a few."

"Well, thank you for stopping by," I said, standing to walk him to the door.

"You're welcome. Can I hug my favorite ex-wife goodbye? I don't want to cause no issues for you and your man."

"Your favorite, I'm the only and you bet not forget that." I said to him.

"And that's the way it'll be for me."

I shook my head at him. "You can have a hug. You won't cause any issues because I'm not going to allow you to give us any." I assured him.

"Understood. Goodbye Tamara Reed." He said before kissing me passionately.

"Ben." I said, after breaking from his kiss. "What are you doing?"

"I wanted to leave you with something to remember me by. We didn't leave off on the best of terms." He said, still holding me. The way he held me close and looked at me said if he could take it there, he would. And if I didn't take a step back, I'd be in trouble. This feeling was too familiar for my comfort.

"Your not playing fair Ben and you know it. This is not right." I said, taking a step back out of his arms.

"Nor was breaking my heart and leaving me, but now we're here." He said, taking a step forward and regaining his hold around my waist. "Look at me. You ran away before, but not this time. This time, you will face me. I played it cool during TJ and Erica's wedding, but I was crushed and I kept my distance. There the two of you were hugged up, laughing, kissing, dancing, and may I add engaged. You didn't think about me not even once. You didn't think about how I would feel to see you with this man? All I could see at the moment was you enjoying your new life with my replacement. It's almost as if I didn't exist to you. Once a upon a time, Tamara, we were in love. We got married. You were my wife. The one I loved more than anything or anyone. Was divorce in our plans, no. But, I settled to have you as a friend in business, and trust me, I'm grateful for that, but we were more, much more. I just needed you to remember that I existed because seeing you interact with him really hurt me. It was like I never was."

He said, before releasing me and walking out the door.

I was so taken aback, I couldn't find any words to say, and maybe that was for the best. The truth is, I had seen him. I knew that he was there, but what could I have done? I saw the disappointment on his face, and also saw when he left. How could I forget him? I fought hard to suppress every feeling that I had for him after we kissed. Despite what he said, I had remembered and that passionate kiss won't let me forget, but what we had was over.

In my heart, we'd said our goodbyes when I picked up the rest of my things. Perhaps this visit was his, and I'm going to try my best to leave it right here. I had no reason to entertain what my head was thinking. I was truly happy with Marcus. I believe that I am in my right place. Ben will always hold a special place in my heart. My thoughts were to reach out to him, to discuss the matter further, to explain my position, but there was no need. His goodbye was

goodbye and so was mine.

Chapter 29

MARCUS

I wanted to surprise Tamara by taking her to dinner, but I couldn't make reservations because the restaurant had been fully booked up for the night. So instead, I planned a night in for us. She was going to be so surprised. I told her that I was on call tonight, but I wasn't. I wanted to do something special for her. I knew how nervous she was this morning. Today was a very big day for her and the staff at the foundation. I loved how she curated a group of experts to service their clients. She claimed it was the brain-child of Phillip, but I could see a lot of her in this project as well. She spared no expense to ensure the comfort and wellness of their clients. I invited a few colleagues to her grand opening, and they were quite impressed. I wasn't surprised by their reactions, whenever Tamara commits herself to something worthwhile it always produces excellent results.

Our dinner had been just delivered from one of our favorite restaurants. All I needed to do was pour the wine. I had just hung up from her. She informed me that she was minutes away from home. I told her that I wished I could be there with her, but would see her soon. I promised her that we were going to have a celebratory dinner, but I hadn't said when. I heard the garage door open. She'll be coming through the door in five, four, three, two, one.

"Babe," she yelled. "Oh, my God! What is all this?" She asked.

"I wanted to surprise you with dinner." I said, hugging her.

"Babe, you didn't have to do all this." She said as she looked around the room.

"Yes, I did. Let it not be said that I don't know how to spoil Mrs. Worthington."

"You got my favorite roses and everything."

"First, I want you to sit down and I'll bring out our

dinner. How was your first day? I want to hear all about it."

I told her before going into the kitchen.

"I can show you better than I can tell you."

"What do you mean?" I asked after returning to sit

our plates down on the table.

She stood and backed me up to the wall. "Girl don't

start." I told her while she kissed me on my neck.

"Not only am I going to start, but I will finish it,

too." She told me.

Before I could say another word, our clothes hit the

floor and our food required reheating. I don't know what

had gotten into her, but she left me speechless. She acted

like a woman possessed. Something in her had awakened,

and it consumed every bit of me. It was wild and

untamable. It begged for more and more. The more I

appeased her, the more insatiable she became. I've never

known her to be this spontaneous, so domineering. She was

on top and controlled me in the way she swiveled her hips.

I took in every ounce of pleasure from watching her and

she knew it, too. She started telling me how I was making

her feel, and what she wanted to do to me, and how she was

going to do it. Knowing how crazy it drove me. Every time

I came close to releasing, she'd change her rhythm to

refuse me. She tortured me like this for what felt like an

eternity. When I had enough of her toying with me, I

flipped her over and ended her sadistic game. There was

nothing left for me to hold back and she was getting ready

to receive it all as we exploded together hard and furious.

Chapter 30

TAMARA

A Year Later...

"Mrs. Worthington, are you enjoying your brunch?" Marcus asked.

"So much that I don't want to leave and go home tomorrow."

"Agreed. Honeymooning in Paris has been incredible, but wherever I am with you would be. Unfortunately, my love, we have to get back to the real world." He said after taking a sip of his coffee.

"Same here. Too bad I can't bring La Maison Rose home with us."

"I know. The food here is so good. I know my mother would love it."

"Speaking of mothers. I don't want to face their wrath when we do return." I confessed.

"Yeah babe, they are pretty pissed with us, but it was our decision not to have an over the top wedding."

"They didn't see it that way. An elopement was not a part of their wedding agenda. I'm just glad that we promised to have a huge reception when we returned, and they could plan it for us." I said.

"Well, at least they hadn't gone overboard in cost. That's all I was concerned about."

"I know what you mean. They had a lot of time to make up for. But I think when we come back with our exciting news, they'll forget all about it. I'm just relieved it wasn't food poisoning like we originally thought. I'm pretty sure they'll forgive us though."

"They certainly will. When they ask about their souvenirs, I'm going to say to them that we brought you all back a baby." He said.

"I'm still shocked, but that's all they'll really want, anyway. Wow, we are really going to be parents. Everyone is going to go crazy. I hadn't even told Erica yet." I said excitedly.

"Let's not tell anyone until we go to the doctor to confirm how far along you are. Once we know that, then we can surprise them with the news, possibly at the reception. Do you know where the festivities are going to be held?"

"Yes, at the Theodore on the Southside."

"Nice. That place is huge. The hospital gave us a Christmas party there one year."

"When mom sent me the pictures of the place, it was very nice. I'm so excited about everything, our growing family and the life that we are building together. Babe, we're so blessed, you know that?"

"I do. I can't thank God enough for what he has blessed me with, and now we are about to have a little one."

"What do you want, a girl or a boy?" I asked him.

"It doesn't matter to me, babe, just as long as he or she is healthy."

"Amen to that. But I think I want a boy. I think I would make a great boy, mom." I said, laughing.

"It's still early in the pregnancy, babe. You may change your mind."

"Nah, it fits me."

" How far along to do believe you are?"

"Maybe a few weeks."

"I think I may know when it happened. After you came home from your first day being at the foundation. That night you couldn't get enough. The next time you have an inspiration like that, can you give a brother a warning? You wore me out! I had to rehydrate and everything. We ended up eating so late that night."

"I had a sexy man waiting at home for me who I had deprived for way too long."

"If you're going to do it like that, deprive me anytime. But give me a warning first," he said, laughing. "Are you ready to go?"

"Yes." I told him. Thankful he didn't ask what had inspired me. Ben's kiss set my body ablaze that day, and since I couldn't call him, Marcus had to be the one to put it out.

My life's journey led me back to where I was always meant to be. I cherish the memories of where I've been, but flourished in where I was. Even with Ben, he had done exactly what he said he would do. He moved and opened a firm in L.A. and found himself another love. Erica couldn't say if they were serious or not, but he seemed very happy, and I loved that for him. The last time I saw him was at our god-daughter's first birthday party. He introduced me to his lady friend as his favorite ex-wife. It was awkward at first for me, because I felt a tinge of jealousy towards her. The thought of him moving on with someone else bothered me, and I know it shouldn't have, but it did. I knew how he felt about me, and to think he no longer had those feelings was unsettling. I had to give it to Ashley, she was as graceful as she was beautiful. In her own laid back way, she laughed off what he said. I don't know if it was the pregnancy hormones or what, but I don't think I could've done that. I'd feel some kind of way. She was definitely different. I wanted so badly not to like Ashley, especially after befriending Erica. TJ was cool, but Erica belonged to me. Her poise told you exactly who she was, but it was her warming demeanor that made me lose any negativity I felt towards her. She made me feel at ease. So much so that I introduced her to my husband, who was not amused by Ben's comment. I cut my eyes at Ben as he smirked, walking by us, trying to avoid eye contact with me. Men and their egos. He knew good and well calling me his favorite anything would annoy my husband.

As A'ja's god-parents, we spoiled her something rotten for her first birthday and Erica and TJ gave us flak about it too, but what were god-parents for if they couldn't spoil their god-children?

"Wait until your little one is born. We're going to return the favor." Erica told me as I was feeding A'ja another cookie. I wasn't worried about her. She had two grandmothers to get past first, and I don't think she wanted no smoke with Cookie Reed.

The crew was back together again, laughing and talking, but things were certainly not the same. We were missing two, Phillip and Kherington. As we all sat there together, there was a brief moment of silence that fell over the table. I guess that was our time to reflect upon the fallen. Ce broke the silence by asking his wife if she would pass him a fork.

"Now, y'all know the after party is going to start after the kids leave, right?" TJ told us.

"And after the party is the after after party." Ce and Ben said in unison.

"No, it won't be either," Erica said. "Y'all going home. I'm tired. And I know you are tired." She said to me.

"I see the conspiracy now. Last year we couldn't have no fun, because you were pregnant. Now, this year, Tamara's pregnant. Felicia, are you planning on becoming pregnant next because y'all got us in a chokehold with this mess? And Ashley, you bet not think about it! I'm on to all of y'all. If our days of fun are over, just say that. Y'all don't have to keep getting pregnant." TJ ranted.

The table erupted in laughter. "Bro, something is really wrong with you." Ce said.

"You know there's a facility not too far from here that you can come in and talk to somebody about these anguish out bursts that you've been having. I hear that it's a pretty good facility." I told him.

"Nawl, nawl. Let me stop talking before y'all have somebody come lock my ass up for real. That's alright, y'all can have as many babies as you want to. I'm going to go have fun by myself."

"You don't have to be alone, friend," Ashley said.

"Nope, that's alright. I don't need no company." He said.

In true TJ fashion, he kept us laughing all night long. I must admit, I missed us all being together. I can see now why Ashley and Erica became fast friends. She was something very special and I'm happy to know Ben is at his best with her. As messy and complicated as things had gotten, business was good, life was great, and the love I shared with my husband was wonderful. I wouldn't change my life for anything or anyone.

Chapter 31

BENJAMIN

It took something traumatic to happen to me to make me grow-up. With all that I had gained and accomplished, I only had one regret, Tamara. I could've stepped-up and fought for her. Kissing her that day told me everything I needed to know in the way she responded back to me. Perhaps had I done so, she would've conceived our child, but instead I did something I'd never thought possible. I let her go. I released Tamara, knowing that I couldn't possibly love another the way I loved her. I'd rather seen her happy and free than to be trapped in misery with me. Her not being able to trust me would've taken its toll on the both of us.

Unselfishly, I loved her from afar, and despite how I felt about her, life went on and so did I. A few months later, I met Ashley at a conference in L.A. She worked for one of the top investment firms there. We exchanged

numbers and had become fast friends. One thing that I

respected about Ashley was her outlook on life. When we

first started dating, she told me that she was not going to

fight with me for a place in my life. She was not the kind of

woman that begged a man for a title. If I wanted her to be

the woman in my life, I had to place her there, and I did.

She accepted me for who and where I was. The

deep admiration I have for her made me want to get closer

to her romantically. I've never met a woman that could

command my attention by the way she moved. Ashley was

a trailblazer in her own right. She didn't allow her looks to

take her places, and although she could because she was

undeniably beautiful, she used her intelligence to get her

into those rooms.

This woman came in and turned my whole world

upside down. She opened my eyes to see that there was

more to life than the mistakes that I had made. So, of

course, I had to marry her. We married in Santa Barbara at the Villa and Vine after dating for two years. Doing life with her made everything I'd been through worth it. What I found in Ashley was irreplaceable. I had someone that not only did I want to do life with, but couldn't do life without. She was my joy, hope, and forever love. I will spend the rest of my life being fulfilled and grateful for the gift God had blessed me with. And just think placing states between Tamara and I led me to the greatest love of my life.

Happily Ever & After.

If you loved this book series, you'll love what's

coming in February 2026.

TOXIC

LOVE

Your review matters!

Please enter your review of this book

online at Amazon.

I'll love to hear from you:

Please email me at

ddmiles.relationshipreflections@gmail.com

Want to read more? See the

link below:

Website at

https://relationshipreflections.org.

www.ingramcontent.com/pod-product-compliance
Lightning Source LLC
Chambersburg PA
CBHW071603110726
47908CB00007B/2230